DO SOMETHING do something DO SOMETHING

joseph riippi

ISBN 13: 978-0-9841025-0-1
ISBN 10: 0-9841025-0-7

First edition.

Published by Ampersand Books
an imprint of Ampersand Press, St. Petersburg, FL.
www.ampersand-books.com

Set in Hoefler Text.

Cover design and illustrations by Chauncey O'Neill.

Grateful acknowledgement is made to the editors of the following publications, in which portions of this book previously appeared in somewhat (or very) different forms:

10,000 Tons of Black Ink
Ampersand Review
The Bitter Oleander
Every Day Fiction
FlatmanCROOKED
The Ink-Filled Page Anthology
The Melancholy Dane
New Delta Review
Promethean
Salamander
Slush Pile Magazine
Soon Quarterly
ZAUM

for L
lovelovelove

tomorrow and tomorrow and tomorrow

'Something about the bird'

It is twenty years ago and the boy looks behind him to make sure no one is watching. He can hear the clatter of silverware and conversations. The adults are all out on the deck, looking at the view, talking about whatever it is adults talk about. The things he's not supposed to know, the boy thinks. No one can see him, and so he turns back to the base of the tree. He pulls the brim of his too-big Mariners cap down far in a guise of secrecy. This bird must have been here for a long time, he thinks. Quiet, fallen. A red-breasted robin frozen in a crucified pose. One wing atwist, asymmetrical, fighting normal avian perfection. Yes, it must have been here a long time, the boy reaffirms, examining the flat needles from the cedar that have settled on and around it, dark greens mixing with the red of the feathers. There's something about the feathers he loves, a loss of coloring, an absence of brightness—the difference between a book borrowed from the library and a book brought home from a store. The boy holds his breath, and looks behind him again. Still no one watching. He creeps even closer to the bird in his squatting stance.

He's never touched a dead thing before. Not something as real as a bird, at least. He's been fishing before, touched fish. But those are food. They're not really real. There was the time his neighbor's dog got hit by a car but he wasn't allowed to go into the street to look at it. Just glimpsed it from the window; the white fur with red stains on it, its head all limp and funny. Now he's scared to touch it, but he sticks his hand out anyway, brushing the cedar needles away with the grain of the feathers, petting the dead thing. It feels just like he thought it would, and that seems wrong. He expected to be surprised. He hears a woman's voice calling his name. He's caught, he thinks. He stands fast and turns to be ready and digs in his head for a lie. Have you seen Eddie? the voice says, further away now. He's safe; he has a little time.

Back in his squat, he reaches beneath the bird, scooping it like he's about to lift water. Why is he so careful not to hurt it? He can't break it, can he? But still he's gentle as he slides his hands under, careful, careful, careful—he gets his small hands all the way under, cradling the bird in his palms now. It feels like nothing. He lifts a wing slightly with one hand, trying to remake its movement, lifting it up and down; but it seems wrong. He can feel the bone in it, unconnected to the rest of the body. The other wing seems fine, but with one broken this bird is monstrous, incorrect. He is holding it close to his face to smell when he hears his name, sharp and loud, and right behind him. He drops the bird, sees it fall so unnaturally and ugly he wants to cry. And then he sees his mother's face, jaw dropped to see such a disobedient child. Her eyes, a blue and a green, wide and amazed. He knows he's not supposed to touch dead things. He's not supposed to know what a dead bird feels like. She towers over him and grabs him by the arm and scolds him, drags him crying to the house where she scrubs his hands and orders him out onto the deck. She tells him to stay where she can see him. To sit still and not to move or do anything. Just sit there, Eddie, she says, and Eddie stops crying and sits. He loves her and will do what she says.

He will sit here and enjoy the beautiful day, the beautiful view, and he will forget what a dead bird feels like.

fig. 1

fig. 2

fig. 3

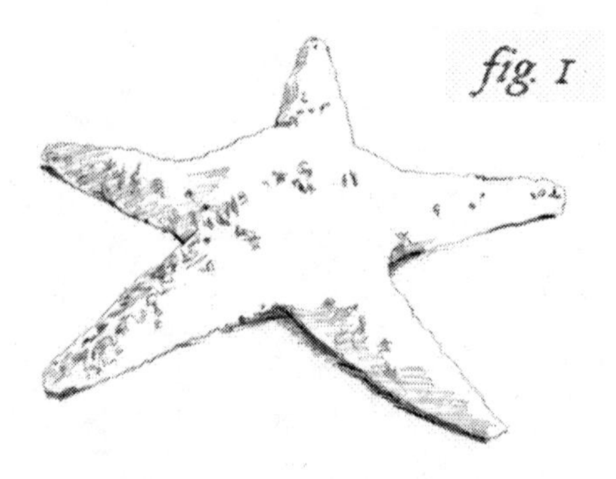

September 10, 2009

Walking into the white tile lobby with her garment bag wheeling behind her and long dark hair in her face and eyes, she thought how she had been in one of these places before too; and she reflected on how, now, despite her seeming like a young, distraught woman about to check herself in, this was her little brother's turn. She had come to the Western State Hospital not because she wanted to, but because she felt she had a responsibility to remind Eddie of her own survival, to show him that a person could really come out on the other side of something like this and live a real life afterwards. She was anxious, too, for what Eddie had done, what had put him here, was not completely unlike what a man had once done to her. But she knew that just by being here she was doing something; it was not a matter of getting *past* what had happened but rather getting *through* it. Of dying one's hair dark, of forgetting a name, of tattooing your body forever with a mark to remind you that no matter how many arms they rip off or how many ribs they shatter, you'll grow back. Like a starfish. She owed it to Eddie to teach him this. She found the young patient in the game room, unshaven and wearing red flannel pajama bottoms and a navy blue Seattle Mariners t-shirt. His thick brown hair curled and tangled, long down to the shoulders. Thick-framed glasses rested at an angle on his nose, a bent stem. Sitting alone in a chair with a thick hardcover book he looked much like the college senior she'd last seen him as, when he had come to visit her in Asheville. He spoke. Hey, S, the boy said, rising from his chair when she entered the room. Your hair's a different color again. She smiled and they hugged, him a full head taller, and she followed him out to a covered porch where they watched cold rain drip through the great pines that enclosed the hospital grounds. Sometimes it rains so cold the trees look blue, her brother said. Not to her it seemed, but rather to himself, and no one else in particular. She placed a scarred hand on his shoulder and left it there. Then she said gently: I'm sorry this happened to you. Roger shouldn't have put you here. She waited for him to say something. A minute passed, rain fell, and her hand stayed on his shoulder. The boy's words were fast and fearful when he spoke: The thing about Sartre, he said, the thing about him is that he was right when he said hell is other people. Because I mean, there's no getting out, because getting out would mean that you're going to be alone, which is a worse hell than Sartre's, because it's a hell where there's nothing to do, just blackness and echoes and your own voice endlessly describing bad memories, assuming you can remember anything at all, and that's why people take drugs I think—for the other perspectives, like another person, another point of view across the table having coffee and chatting. He stopped, and stared out the window at the cold blue landscape before looking down and starting again. Drugs can make it so it's like you're in both places, he said. Both sides of the table, a table spinning, and I think the fire part of hell is the fear that, for eternity, there's always something worse to come, and that's the loneliness, the uncertainty. Loneliness, her brother said, holding up the thick book in his hands. Loneliness and silence and fire. The girl with the starfish tattoo kept her hand on her brother's shoulder for a moment after he finished. She watched his legs bouncing up and down at the knees, the book resting on his lap and his hands fisted together on top of it. When she removed her hand they sat together without saying anything. She hadn't known he was this bad, this frightened, this far away. She remembered the feeling herself and the starfish clutched at her chest like a burn. Finally, when it was dark out and time for her to go, she approached the front-desk nurse and requested the name of a nearby motel. She was given directions and left to walk the quarter-mile to the motel alone, under glowing streetlamps that lit the rain to look like sepia needles. Memories fell with the rain and the starfish held her left breast over her heart. She had no umbrella as she approached the small Ramada Inn; her garment bag dripped on the hard carpet in the lobby, and the sleeve of her sweater smeared the ink on the forms when she gave her signature at the check-in. The old man behind the counter swiped her credit card and shook his head at her aloneness, her smallness and femaleness. In the small, antibacterial-scented room she watched a highway through the screened window, wet headlights veining past an army base that rested still and eerie among the evergreens. Even in the dark she thought that her brother was right, and the trees here could indeed look blue. She shivered and crawled under the stiff sheets for the first of three nights. On the third day she took a cab to a downtown Tacoma bookstore Eddie sent her to, and she bought as much as she could afford and carry off a list he'd written. Maybe you should read something a little lighter, she suggested when she came back with a heavy sack. He laughed at that. Something that's just a nice story, she said, something that could maybe get you out of your head for awhile. Then he stopped laughing and shook his head, furious, from side to side; he nearly shouted, I don't want to get out of my head! I'm in here to stay! He took the books, frantic, and reordered them, alphabetical, into a stack. He set this stack next to another, higher, on the floor next to his thin bed. He thrust out his arm to explain the piles: Done, not done, he pointed. Then he sat on the floor and rubbed his face with his hands and breathed deep in and out. She kept standing and didn't do anything. After a few moments he stood up. Have I showed you what I'm writing? She shook her head no, and again moving fast he showed her his notebooks. They were small and brown, pocket-sized, the same brand that she would take to concerts in college when she wrote music reviews for the university paper. He had done that when he was in college, too, despite his knowing what had happened to her and what had made her stop that part of her life and move to North Carolina. Now, each of the notebooks he kept here in the hospital bore a label of masking type with a name. She saw, *Something About This Room, Something About Sontag, Something About Rain, Something About Politics, Something About The Bird, Something About Blue Trees.* My psych doc's a Freudian, I think, the patient-brother told her. The old school kind. She knows I was critic in college, and she brings me books and notebooks so long as I let her read what I write. The girl with the starfish tattoo looked at the young critic. He's just 24 years old, she thought. How could Roger leave him here? And then she remembered the call from Roger, her step-father, as she had sat alone in the bathroom of her Asheville apartment. Eddie attacked a stripper with the bottom half of a scotch glass, Roger had said. You can deal with that if you want. Roger gave her the address of the hospital outside Seattle and, just like that, he hung up. She looked down at Eddie sitting on the bed now and pulled an orange plastic chair near him, sitting too. So are they like journals? she asked. He shook his head. No, not really. Well, maybe. I don't know. If there's something I see or something that I want to tell the doc about I start writing until, I don't know, it seems like I'm done writing about whatever it was—but usually they end up being about something else by the end. And does that help? she asked. He shrugged. I don't know. But I'm doing something, and that's the key, that's what I write on the back of each of my journals. Do something, do something, do something. He pounded the palm of his hand against his thigh and repeated the words. He sat there, quiet for a moment. They could hear a delivery truck pull up outside the boy's window, its tires hissing against the rainy asphalt. Then he asked the girl with the starfish tattoo, Did it help you? Writing? and she felt the arms of the blue starfish grip her tight on the breast, a burning grip where the bartender had kicked her six years before and where his Conversed foot had broken three of her ribs. She touched the starfish gently and took a breath. The heat and grip receded, as she'd learned it would, and she told the boy, No, it didn't, not really. The night it all happened, when I went to the bar, I'd been writing that night. So when I tried to write afterwards it was hard to separate the one from the other...I don't know if that makes sense. She laughed, nervous. I stopped caring about writing anyway, at least about music writing. The boy's stepsister stood and walked around the small room. She opened the book at the top of the DONE pile. Letters between two writers she'd never heard of. He looked up at her. Do you still *not* write? he asked. She closed the book. No, she said. Well. Yes. No. I don't know. When I was in the hospital at home, at Northwestern, there was a girl who had set herself on fire. She did it in her living room. I forget her name. We used to have to go to these group sessions, all the girls. She always told the same story, about her father who used to beat her and rape her in the night. Most of the girls there had something like that that'd been done to them. But her father had been a Vietnam vet and would have these flashbacks. He would wake up screaming in the night and think she was some villager, and he would go into her room and tie her up and do things to her that were worse than anything I'd ever heard, things with tools and a routine. One night he was passed-out drunk with the History Channel on, like he'd always been, and that night she sat down on the rug between him and the front door, before he could wake up, before he would do that to her again, and she covered herself with kerosene from an old lantern of his father's and she lit a match. The neighbors saw the flash from next door, the giant WHOOSH!!! the girl called it, and they got her out but not the father. Her face was this one amazing scar and she told that story every time we had group. She used to talk about how, when she lived with her father, she never had a real life that was hers, and now that he was dead, she didn't know what to do, and...anyway. She helped me. That story helped me; she was strong. So fucking strong. The girl with the starfish tattoo looked at her brother. He was staring at the linoleum floor. She thought: I wonder if he will ever get out of here. She thought: He's worse off than I'd been. That's a good story, her brother said finally. Then he looked up at her and pointed at the window. It started raining again, he said. You should check if your flight is delayed. Then he stood and they hugged each other. I love you, Eddie, she said. I love you too, S, he said. He handed her a small notebook with *Something About The Blind Man* penciled on the cover. Here's something for the plane. Maybe you can figure me out. He smiled and they hugged again and she walked out crying into the rain, where the trees had stopped looking so blue, and she wondered how he would ever be able to get through this life alone.

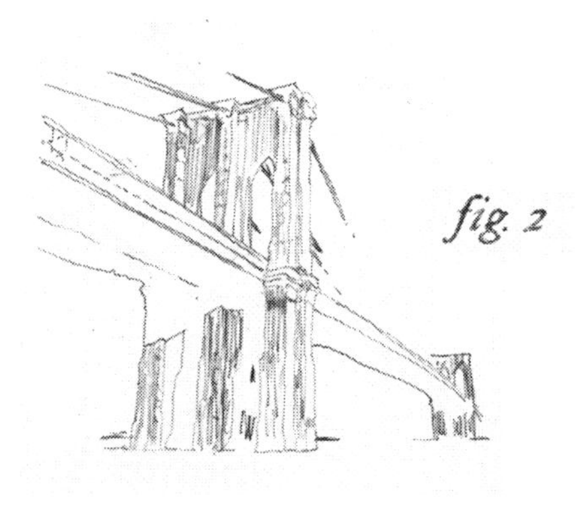

September 10, 2009

At 2:43 in the morning the playwright stumbles out of the bar on Beekman Street across from the South Street Seaport in lower Manhattan. Fucking good time, he drawls, and the soberer friend, the photographer in the dark velvet jacket and CBGBs t-shirt behind him, nods and laughs in agreement. We'll do it again when I'm back in town, the playwright says, and the two of them stand on the sidewalk and laugh some more and shake each other's hand. Then the playwright bends his tall, lanky frame, coughing, his long hands on his knees, and the photographer laughs and stumbles past him into the street to flag down a yellow cab on its way to the FDR drive. Ah fuck man, the playwright moans, spitting between his feet. Hey, what's that fucking Hart Crane poem about the Brooklyn Bridge? He stands up, teetering, and holds a hand to his forehead as if blocking the sun. Hart Crane! he shouts toward the massive silhouette of the great bridge, Hart! Where are you, Hart! The photographer laughs and leans against the open door of the cab. You want a ride uptown? he asks, but the playwright waves him off with a long arm, still gazing east into the sky. Did he really just yell that? Most of the time he can tell where the play in his head ends and his action begins; his mind is split, usually, between thoughts and actions—sometimes they blur, whatever holds them together disappears. And now the bridge rises before him like an enormous brick wall, and he imagines himself up there, standing high and glorious above the city, the great Atlantic in the distance, and he sees himself as an heroic playwright looking down, looking back at the drunken self doing this imagining. What this Martin Patrick Simon's life must look like from that distant, more objective place:

PHOTOGRAPHER *standing in front of the cab,* PLAYWRIGHT *swaying drunk, staring at* BRIDGE.
PHOTOGRAPHER: Well hey, Marty, good luck in Seattle.
PLAYWRIGHT: *Not taking eyes off bridge.* Right, right. Thanks, Davey.
PHOTOGRAPHER: You ought to get out to this gallery in Belltown. I had a show there when I was teaching at the U. I'll send you the address, I forget where it was exactly...somewhere on second avenue.
PLAYWRIGHT: *Belching.* Right, right, will have to do that.
PHOTOGRAPHER: You taking the train then?
PLAYWRIGHT: *Staring back at* BRIDGE, *swallowing.* Yeah, sure. Fulton Street stop's right around here somewhere.
PHOTOGRAPHER: *Holding his hand out*

for a handshake. PLAYWRIGHT *is lost in deep thought, doesn't reach for it.* PHOTOGRAPHER *drops his hand.*

PHOTOGRAPHER: *Sarcastic.* Alright then, Mr. Simon. Maybe next time you get the check, eh?

PLAYWRIGHT *continues staring at bridge.* Take it easy, Davey.

PHOTOGRAPHER: Yup.

Exit PHOTOGRAPHER *into* CAB. *Exit* CAB.

Martin squints and peers at his watch, the hands faintly glow-in-the-dark. Six hours till take-off, he thinks. He wanders down the street mumbling song lyrics to himself. Another yellow cab slows on its way east and he waves it away. Too fucking EXPENSIVE! he shouts. Everything, he thinks, everything is too fucking expensive. At the corner he lights a cigarette (too fucking expensive) and gazes up at the dense buildings and dark, expansive apartments of the empty financial district (too fucking expensive). 2:47 am now, a Tuesday in September, 2009. Where the fuck is Fulton Street? he mutters, and then again in the tune of the Clash song stuck in his head. *Should I stay or should I go...where the fuck is Fulton Street.* He keeps his feet trudging west, knowing the train has to be somewhere in the opposite direction of the water. *Where the fuck is Fulton Street...Should I stay or should I go.* He glances behind to make sure he's headed inland, and he sees hanging from the side of a brick building a blue pine tree, neon and buzzing and glowing, a sign for a new bar or restaurant. Well that's the wrong fucking color, he thinks, and, looking back to the Brooklyn bridge, rising tall and dark and monumental against the sky, he conjures the new image of himself; *this* Martin Patrick Simon is a new character, he thinks, a divorced, broken character—a man-of-letters; yes, he is a man-of-his-own, a man walking in an empty, wet, and drunken street, in an inebriated state (no, an *enlightened* state!) and talking to no one but staring, yes, staring and defying (no, *challenging*!) the great bridge, and, like the great heroes of Herodotus, the great heroes of Plato and Virgil and Euripides, shouting to the gods: MELVILLE WIPED THE FUCKING FLOOR WITH YOU, CRANE! WIPED THE FUCKING *FLOOR!* He lets these words echo back and forth in his head, and the great hero-playwright chuckles, turns his back on the bridge, and keeps walking west. West, always west from now on, he says, swelling with his newfound heroism, and with still no one listening he belches, he farts, he feels in his pockets for an antacid to cover the taste of faint vomit in the back of his throat. He has to remember to pack Tums for the flight the next morning, he reminds himself, breaking his trance, falling away from the grandiloquent place atop the bridge's height. Yes, he says, fully to himself, suppressing a burning and painful belch, I must remember to pack Tums.

fig. 3

September 15, 2009

'Something about the Blind Man'

This place is supposed to be calm, Spivey—I know you hate it when I call you that...what did you say it was? Disrespectful? Sorry, DOCTOR SPIVEY. (But would you prefer Nurse Ratched? I mean honestly; surely that would be less respectful). So: I want an explanation. It's that fucking blind man, the new guy. It's been two nights in a row now that that fucking television has been on past lights out. And it's not just 'on,' but it's on loud as a fucking rave in hell. Voices—voices like screaming cadavers coming out of the walls, Spivey. —like Rimbaud said, 'The dawn is harsh, to say the least.' I can't tell what they're saying, but I'm still awake when Rimbaud's dawn shows up. Each of the past two nights, when there's the lights out call, and the silence, there's suddenly the television. I close my eyes and press my head into the pillow but it's like I can SEE the sound Spivey—sound waves like snakes, like great black serpents erupting from the hot mouth of a volcano, slithering down the slopes with their mouths open and fangs pointed and coming for me fast, while all the while, eyes still closed, I can see the blind man just sitting there not seeing not looking at anything but just listening, listening, listening to the wretched sounds he's making and torturing me with, and I want to run and kill him, to cut out his sightless eyes, but more I just want to sleep! I am supposed to learn to be calm here Spivey! I would kill for just a cigarette, for a drink, for SOMETHING, but I am trying, Spivey, I am trying to sleep every night in a ball on the bed like it used to work when I was a kid and I would cover my head with my blue blanket and press my face into the pillow when I had nightmares and so last night I moved my bed to the center of the room where I hoped the noise and the snakes couldn't reach through the walls to get me but then I thought about Melville and I thought about Tashtego's fist grabbing that bird as the Pequod sank that beautiful image and I know thinking of myself as the bird I know I know I know that's irrational (even crazy I can still see the irrationality in an image) but when I'm sleepless and the TV is SO FUCKING LOUD!! I can't think. I can't think at all, and it hurts, it hurts, it fucking HURTS. But to the point: I asked one of the nurses today and he wouldn't tell me anything. I haven't seen the blind man himself except for in the nights but you must be able to do something. Please, SPIVEY: there are voices coming out of my walls, just fucking PLEASE STOP IT!!! so I can think, so I can concentrate on figuring out what I have to do to get out of this. I am crying as I write this, Spivey. Your patients shouldn't have to cry to get what they need. That's poor attention. Poor Ratchedian treatment.

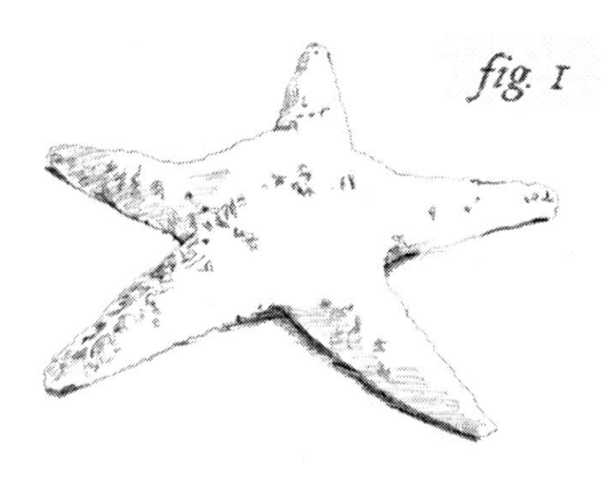

fig. 1

The girl with the starfish tattoo walked through a cold jetway to the door of the Boeing 737, flight CO 1480 from Seattle-Tacoma International to Newark Liberty International. From Newark she would catch a connection back to North Carolina and Asheville. She settled into the window seat with her purse and bottle of water. She put the water in the back pocket of the seat in front of her, held her purse in her lap, and thought about her step-brother and the hospital she'd just left. Yes, she had spent a month in a center like that after an overdose of antidepressants, but Eddie had problems beyond what she'd had. Hers had been rooted outside herself. She could blame the bartender, yes, and she could blame her past self's decisions—but she'd learned from what had happened. She'd learned something before she became a girl with a starfish tattoo, a tattoo to remind her that, no matter what happens, she can grow back, just as a starfish can regenerate an arm. Eddie's problems, though, they were *in* him, in his brain, and that couldn't just fix itself. Something wasn't connected right and he would dissociate; things could be perfectly normal and then could scare him to the point of an anxiety attack. He could quite literally, the doctor told her, scare himself to death if he didn't stay heavily medicated. From between the straps of her purse she removed a linen jacket, leaving the notebook Eddie had given her in the bag and sliding it all under the seat in front of her. From the pocket of her jacket she removed headphones and a small iPod. She used the jacket as a blanket and leaned her head back and stared out the window. Eddie would be okay, she told herself. For all Roger's shit, he'd put Eddie in a good hospital, and the drugs were starting to work. Eddie just has to realize they can work. He just has to let them do what they do, the woman who reads his notebooks said. He's making good progress, but as his sister, it would be good if you could come back—he trusts you; that's very clear from what he's written. The girl with the starfish tattoo thought about these words while the music played softly in her headphones, and she wondered what her brother's dreams must be like, what sort of terrorizing nightmares he must suffer through. She was wondering this, and thinking of her own nightmares too, as she adjusted her head against the side of the plane, and fell into a deep sleep.

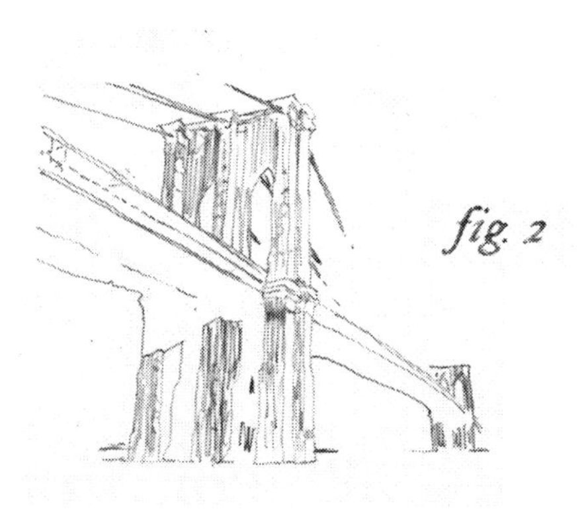

His shoes make squishing noises, wet from puddles, and his fingernails are blackened from mis-struck matches. He's walked now for fifteen, twenty minutes, and still Martin hasn't found the Fulton Street station. Isn't this west? Where is he? Now he decides he has gone too far; he has passed Fulton to either the north or the south, and so he heads south to where he knows Wall Street will be eventually. The station stairs he climbed earlier this evening descend into the pavement just in front of the Trinity Church, right in front of Alexander Hamilton's grave, and that will be at the end of Wall Street. It had occurred to him then, walking up those stairs, that the subway has always seemed like some sort of mass grave to him, and it's thoughts like that that have helped make the decision to leave the city easier. This time tomorrow he will be in Seattle, sleeping on a friend's couch, a legitimate Northwest theater director, not just another moderately self-sufficient New York playwright. A writer-director, he'll be, and he imagines it, saying, This will be good. Trudging along toward Wall Street, he repeats, This will be good, this will be good, and as he told the producer: Finally I'm going to do something, do something, do something! pounding his fist on the desk. With this move he'll leave New

York behind, a city he's never loved, and he'll leave Claire behind, an ex-wife he still loves, but mostly he will leave Anna behind, their daughter that didn't live long enough to see the outside of the hospital, dying instead just 16 days after being born. So Martin will work, and he will make a new home on the other side of the country, away from memories and the storm that ensued after the 17th day, when he and Claire told the doctors to rip out the tubes keeping Anna technically alive and went back to their apartment, which could never be a home after that. Martin makes a right at Wall Street and sees the Trinity Church façade, lit golden from lamps as strategic as a theater's, rising a half-mile away at the end of a concreted canyon corridor. This is the way home. He'll walk this last half-mile, catch a train, sleep a few hours, catch a cab, a plane, another cab, and he'll be home. He hasn't had a home in years, it seems, and he pauses for a moment to let a police car pass, takes a deep breath and steps up onto the curb. That's when it hits him like a bullet: a sharp pain in his stomach, the seafood dinner clenching his guts like clawed, flaming fists that burn all the way through the coils of his intestines. The playwright bends double, fighting the urge to release it all. He looks around, frantic, and wants to run, somewhere, anywhere, but any movement is a risk. Sweat on his forehead, sweat on his cheeks and back. Wall Street at 3:12 am is a desert, is a ghost town, is closed. There has to be a bar, a Starbucks, a blue neon tree, something with a toilet. He stands upright and takes a deep breath. He makes it four steps before a sword seems to stab down his throat and out his lower back. He is conscious of groaning, loud, as invisible adders coil and clench inside him. He imagines himself and tries to change what he sees. He stands again and this time expects the pain and meets it head on. He turns onto a side street away from the church and the subway—the train will take too long, he knows, and he needs to find something now to get rid of this—so he runs, his shoes squishing. He runs, runs.

fig. 3

Help me god help me Spivey. It's the middle of the night and they're here and I know who they are. it's the snakes all around, the snakes with their mouths open are talking now, all of them talking and screaming in the same voices, over and over, forever, always, the same insane voices I'm hearing now loud as a fucking rock concert but clear and terrifying. it's newscasters, newscasters, newscasters. I know their voices. they're right here. they're right next to me. the same newscasters, over and over. the same two minutes of news over and over. it's september 11. Not the september 11 of last week but the sept 11 of 8 years ago, planes and towers and fire, 2001, and a man's voice is talking about the first tower being hit and then a woman interrupts and announces that the second tower has just been hit and there's a plane spivey there's a plane coming for me. spivey please they're announcing it there's a plane they're announcing it.

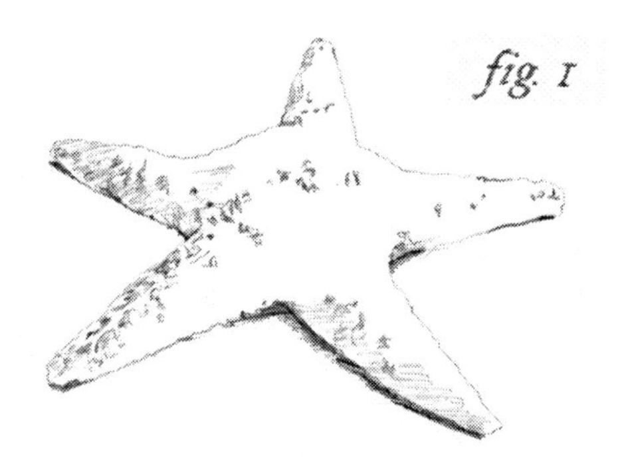

She was hearing nothing but the soft chords of Leonard Cohen's guitar when the husband and wife, McDonald's bags and carry-ons in tow, came down the aisle grunting and bumping into armrests and arms and shoulders. The husband was the leader with the luggage; the wife dutifully following with red and white paper sacs glowing translucent with grease. The girl with the starfish tattoo leaned closer to the window and pulled down the armrest, hoping they would either sit in front of her or continue on to all the rows left behind her in the back of the plane. She closed her eyes to seem sleeping. She could picture it: two excited, senior travelers, overweight and anxious, ready for their trip to the Big Apple and bus tours and Broadway—but most of all ready to talk to their neighboring passengers about it. She pretended to sleep and listened to her music. Then: the husband was tapping her on the shoulder. Miss? he said. He sniffed and rubbed his nose. I think these are ours? he asked, pointing to the two seats. Are you 14A? The girl with the starfish tattoo nodded. So these must be B and C then? he asked again, still sniffing, leaning closer than most people would to show her the boarding passes. Get the fuck off my arm rest, she wanted to say; but instead said only, I think so, yes. The husband nodded, and then checked his stubs against the small dome light hanging from the overhead compartment, the light that labeled the row and seat numbers just as she'd said they were. He announced with pride to his wife that they were in the right place. Told you we'd find it! he exclaimed, and the wife just nodded. After putting their bags into the overhead he lowered his fleshy self into the center seat and leaned toward the girl again. He put a hand on her shoulder. You'll have to excuse us, he said, almost whispering, We haven't flown in years. My wife is very nervous, you know, since 9/11. The girl with the starfish tattoo nodded again, polite, and looked past to the woman sitting with an overflowing purse in her lap, wringing the leather of the straps in her wrinkled hands. The girl with the starfish tattoo closed her eyes again, put her head against the window, and covered her nose with her hand as the man unwrapped his double-quarter-pounder with cheese and fumbled with a ketchup packet.

fig. 2

Sweat pours oily and thick down Martin's face as he searches the passing storefronts. He passes restaurants and Starbucks, glass doorways he knows he has entered over the years he's lived in this city, but now covered with iron grates and bars. He thinks of running back to the bar, to the restaurant that served him the ciopino and beers and whiskey that started this all. They are the rightful owners of what is coming, he thinks, they are the ones to blame for this. But he has come too far to go back, and he doesn't remember passing anything that might offer relief since the blue tree —if he had seen something he would have asked for directions to the Fulton Street stop. Now he thinks his best move is to find a subway station, any station, and hide behind the dumpsters at the end of the platform and squat for thirty seconds. He can get out whatever comes in the first wave, then pull up his pants and get to his apartment before there is a second or a third. But he's taken too many turns and he's lost the Trinity Church, the golden light to home. Even a cab would be salvation, just a cab that could take him to the nearest open door, but every cab that's passed has been occupied, and not many have passed. He starts to pray. An Our Father, then a Hail Mary. Suddenly he makes a turn and sees neon at the end of the block. He makes promises to the Catholic God of his youth as he approaches—the masses he'll attend, the tithes he'll give—but he reaches only another iron gate. Shit. He lets the promises to God hang in the air. Hell is not other people, he thinks, hell is the absence of a toilet when you need it. Sartre was never in this situation. He moves on. Then: Wall Street again, a Great Wall of salvation. He runs, takes a risk and lets out a fart but feels liquid, terror, a burning itch and the tightening of the seafood clench around his gut. He looks up the street and sees the Trinity Church, golden again, closer now, and he goes to run but in his movements liquid pours free into his boxer-briefs. He is too late, he thinks, he has to do it now. He doubles over, a hand on the steps of Federal Hall, the great columned building where George Washington was inaugurated as president. The stern bronze likeness of this better George W. looks past Martin, the humble citizen, to a sleeping New York stock exchange. Martin climbs the steps on all fours towards the relative safety of the Hall's columns, and at the top he collapses against one of them, an itching heaviness in his pants. He notices movement behind him and peers. Patrolling the entrance to the stock exchange, two policemen with rifles and body armor have their backs to him. He is breathing hard, panicking, and he feels more liquid rush as he attempts to stand; he tries not to cry as sweat drips from his face into his already swampy shirt. He crawls into a corner at the top of the stairs and, fumbling, pulls down his jeans and squats. A burning spray like a torch blasts onto the marble. Relief. He sighs. His body instantly cools. Then at once it all turns to burning and an unreal pain that lets him whatever mistakes he's made are still not done with him. Then a noise. A voice he can't understand, loud, near. What the SHIT! it booms, as if breaking through the walls of Federal Hall and biting him in the face. On the street the policemen have heard the voice too and turn towards the steps. Martin, squatting, stares at the two homeless men he had not noticed before, the two men who had also taken refuge here behind the George Washington statue and the high marble columns. They rise from their cardboard beds like ghosts and step toward Martin in full view of the now running policemen with their weapons ready. With faces equal parts fear, hate, and incomprehension the homeless men stare, and Martin can only laugh, weep, and continue to squat as, with great pain, he empties himself of everything he has.

fig. 3

Announces was the wrong word for what happened. But calm, Spivey, I will be calm writing this, and I am trying, Spivey, but I don't know how I am supposed to handle this. Here in your hospital and in these "something" notebooks I've got nothing to do but think, nothing to do but get lost in my head. And Thomas DeQuincey, when he was writing his Opium-eater confessions, he once wrote that the human brain is a mighty palimpsest, a palimpsest of everlasting layers—ideas, images and feelings. That reminds me of when I was a little kid, a child, and I used to sneak into my parents bed after they'd woken up, and I would hide inside all those blankets and sheets they had, sneaking around and wriggling around like a little snake myself, and I thought how cold they must have been, to have needed all those blankets. I had only the one blue blanket my mom left me before she died and that always seemed like enough and it still feels like enough, but after what we talked about yesterday I think there are a lot of sheets in my head, and they're fucking tangled, because if you were telling me the truth this morning, and the blind man isn't really real, that there is no television on at night, it is quiet, it is night-as-it-should-be-and-you-are-sure-of-that, that it's me, you say, it's me that's been getting complaints from the neighbors, and it's me who's been screaming in my bed under a little blue blanket, me that makes the most noise and keeps the others up, the others who, like me, are just trying to get well—if that's true, what you say, then what the fuck am I supposed to say? What the fuck am I supposed to do after hearing something like that about myself? I'm imagining it all? I'm "blind to what's real"? Look, I've read Oliver Sacks, too, Spivey, I'm not an idiot, I know what auditory delusions are. You forget, Spivey, you forget that I'm not an idiot. I've read as much as you and I've read the right fucking books so you can't surprise me. You were nice and said they were lucid dreams (you could have said hallucinations) but dreams that we need to talk about, that I need to write about—and you say that that writing will help us (US, you actually said, like we're fucking teammates) and you said that that will help us find the root of the problem and that we will be able to fix it and that then I will be able to get out of here and back to my life. I'll be able to, quote, 'associate properly,' end quote. You say I need to trust the medication. But I don't even know that what I see/hear/feel is real! How can I trust? Sontag says that, as critics, we have to learn to hear more, see more, feel more. So what, am I doing that TOO well??? Why would I dream of September 11? Why would I imagine a blind man listening to videos of newscasters? I DON'T KNOW!!!! IS THAT OKAY??? TO NOT KNOW??? I wasn't there! I know it's one of those things like Kennedy getting shot and I'm supposed to remember exactly where I was when I heard and exactly what I was doing but I don't have a fucking clue. So honesty? You want honesty? I probably slept through it. But let me imagine what you're going to say, what wisdom you're going to bestow upon me from your great majestic and objective height of heroic medical assistance: It's guilt—that's what you're going to say. It's because I wasn't involved that my mind makes me want to BECOME involved somehow, to have a sort of delusion of grandeur thing and be a part of something bigger than myself. And that's the kind of fucking cliché psychoanalysis that's right up your alley, Spivey. And oh, right, I was trying to remain CALM. Well fuck you. You hear me? FUCK YOU!!!!

It is a terrifying thing to believe in something that isn't there. You can't know how terrifying that is. You don't know.

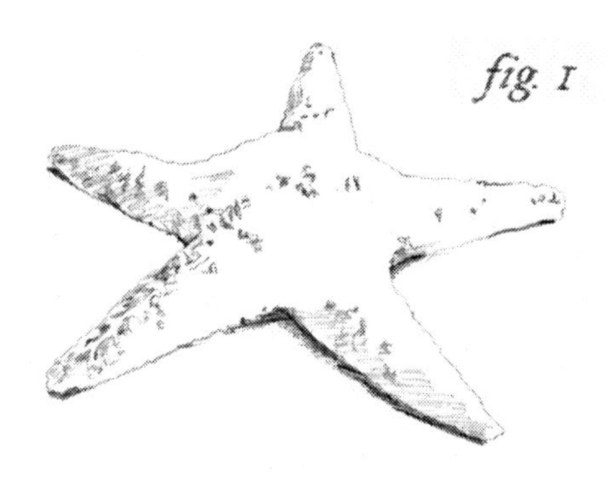

The husband clicked together his seatbelt while the girl with the starfish tattoo listened to her iPod and stared out the window. The husband kept bumping her as he attempted to make himself smaller for the seat, and she tried to imagine what this man's dreams must have been like at her age, what his life has been like. He wore a blue hat with the name of an aircraft carrier on the front. He was probably in the Navy at my age, she thought, or just out of the Navy, and she pictured the husband and his wife on one of the bus tours through downtown Manhattan, taking photos as they passed Ground Zero and the stock exchange, buying t-shirts and going to more expensive versions of the same chain restaurants they love at home. Now, as they sat in their row waiting for the plane to taxi, the wife removed a purple and worn trade paperback from her purse. Then she stood and put the purse in the overhead. Sitting again, she said aloud, to no one in particular, Someone might take it. Munching his French fries the husband nodded in agreement. The wife rose and retrieved the purse, putting her jacket in the overhead instead. Then she sat again, adjusted her seatbelt, and sighed loudly before standing once more to retrieve the jacket and leave the overhead empty. In the aisle, final passengers were boarding. The girl with the starfish tattoo closed her eyes and tried to focus on the music in her headphones, hoping to fall asleep until they reached their cruising altitude, when she could buy a drink. Another song went by before she felt the husband tapping her shoulder. A flight attendant was there, motioning for those in the exit rows to pay attention. The girl with the starfish tattoo removed her headphones and faced the flight attendant so that she could nod, yes, she's happy to help, she can open the door, etc. The husband, like only the rarest of passengers, reached for the card in the seat pocket that detailed the emergency exit row responsibilities and procedures. Then the wife grabbed her husband by the arm and nearly screamed. She made a sound instead that came out more like a cough, staring with horror at a small man with dark skin walking down the aisle. He was speaking into an iPhone, had a thin beard, and carried a small leather briefcase in the hand not holding the phone to his ear. As he approached row 14 he laughed and smiled at whatever was being said on the other end of his conversation, while checking the lights on the overhead compartments to find 12 C, the exit row seat directly in front of the wife. The wife looked from the man to the exit door, from the exit door to the man, and it was clear to her that from his seat he could easily reach over, pull a latch on the emergency door, and bring down the plane. He could kill them all as soon as they were in the air. The flight attendant glanced at the wife when she made the cough-like sound, but then continued in the memorized safety speech. The wife hissed at the husband, Do something! But the husband shushed her, and she clenched his arm tighter, tears building up on her lower eyelids. Do something! Do something! The flight attendant stopped mid-sentence and looked at the wife.

Is everything okay, Ma'am? she asked. The wife pointed at the back of the seat in front of her and screeched, I...I will not...I will NOT fly ONE MILE until that man is CHECKED! For... for...FOR EVERYTHING!!

fig. 2

Martin sits in the back of the police cruiser, blood on his forehead, vomit between his legs. His ass burns from the rash forming there. He had tripped when he stood too quickly with his pants still around his ankles and stumbled down the steps bare-assed and crashing face first into the marble. He rolled and came to rest near the feet of George Washington's statue and almost on top of the feet of a police officer with a loaded M-16. The cop just stood there, before saying to his partner beside him, What. The. Fuck. It wasn't long before Martin was loaded into the back of a squad car and told to wait while that officer and others sorted everything out. The homeless men had to be moved, and something had to be done about the mess behind the columns before the streets filled in a few hours. I have a flight to catch, Martin tried telling them, I'm moving to Seattle, I'm going to be a writer-director and now things are going to be different! I'M GOING TO DO SOMETHING! But they didn't listen. Sitting in the cop car now he reflects on how this is the first time he has ever been arrested for anything, and how little he cares that it is happening; and he thinks how much he hated his life before he decided that everything needed to change. He thinks back on what has brought him to this place, to the backseat of this police car, and he wonders if Anna is looking down on him, if she can see the father who wished she would die when the doctor told him that if she lived she would be brain damaged; if she can see the father who actually told the doctor to rip out the tubes without asking his wife; if she can see the father now experiencing a sadness deeper and thicker than he has ever felt before.

I am the blind man. I see it now, I see myself as the blind man, unable to see, only able to hear. Yes, I am the blind man of the Raymond Carver story, drunk and drawing a cathedral on a ripped paper sac. And yes, I am the blind James Joyce fumbling with Finnegan's crayons. Yes, I am the blind man who went crazy, because I wasn't blind when a plane hit one tower and I was in the other, and I was able to get out but so many others couldn't. Yes, I was in one tower and watched a plane coming low in over the city and I watched it like someone watches a hail mary pass at a football game. the arcing of the head, the eyes following it and...touchdown. Yes, I could see then, and I watched and saw the plane as it shattered into a million pieces and the black cloud and the fuel spilled and I was under it and I was looking up and it burned out my eyes. it was the last thing I saw, thank god, so I didn't see what happened after. But it was the last thing I saw, god damn it, so I didn't see where she went. She, Anna, the love of my life, the one I scream for every night and the one I listen for in the newscasts. The plane was the last thing I saw, so I didn't see all the other people, that army of New Yorkers gray as stone, marching like burnt pillars of salt up Broadway, out of Gomorrah, back to the apartments that could never be homes again after that. It made others a different kind of blind when they looked back too often and saw the marching masquerade, saw that ter-

rible ticker-tape parade of fire and rocks, and the towers crashing like the inside of a volcano around them, black snakes escaping from the rubble to terrorize their dreams, following them and following them, wherever they were going and wherever they went, forever.

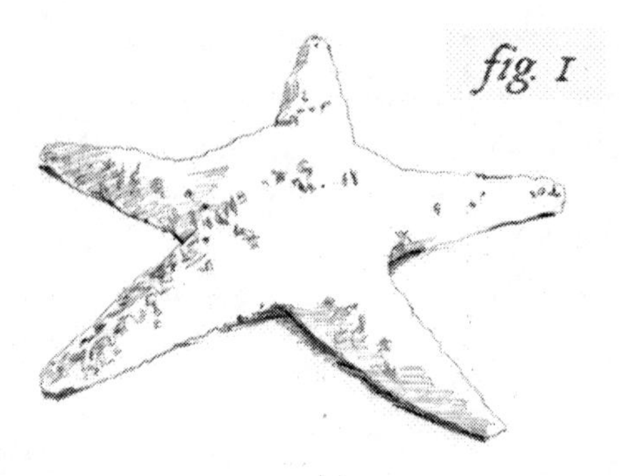

fig. 1

After the wife shouted what she shouted, the girl with the starfish tattoo, the flight attendant, the husband and the others in the emergency exit row just stared at her. The dark-skinned man excused himself from the laughing conversation he'd been having on his phone, turned, and stared. With faces mixed equally with fear, hate, and incomprehension, they all stared. The wife continued to point, trembling, at the dark-skinned man staring back at her, until her husband reached out and lowered her arm. Everything became silent and still. The husband and wife held onto each other. The flight attendant and co-pilot spoke to the husband and wife. The wife was crying and the husband was near shouting with a fearful voice. He kept demanding proof that the man was an American—But why don't you just check him? the husband kept saying, his arms around the shaking wife—while the man himself was led forward by another flight attendant and given a new seat in first class and an apology from the crew. As he got up from his seat he looked at the girl with the starfish tattoo. She smiled a small smile as if to say, I'm not with them and I am oh so sorry that you had to go through that. She thought the man looked as if he were about to cry. She put her headphones back on and looked out the window as the husband continued to argue and the wife continued to cry. She listened to music and tried not to think about anything at all, but it was difficult to do that.

fig. 2

The squad car moves slowly with Martin in the back and they pass the Trinity Church and its centuries-old graveyard. The façade continues to glow golden, his beacon, and Martin wonders when he will ever see it again. Then he wonders if he will make it to Seattle or if he is going to jail. He doesn't care; it doesn't matter. He is starting over tomorrow, today. This is a new life, he has decided. The move, the job. He's shit out his past. But then he closes his eyes and remembers his daughter. He thinks that it's true what they say in plays and movies: I'd give anything for just one more day with her. He pictures the actor playing him:

> PLAYWRIGHT: *head in hands.* I'd give anything for just one more day with her. *(sobbing).*
> I'd give all my life's saving for one more hour.
> *Lights dim.*
> *Curtain.*

fig. 3

I listen to the video tapes now because I am blind and I don't know where she went. I am listening for her. she disappeared. there was a black cloud, an explosion, and she was somewhere nearby when that happened and someone grabbed me and pulled me away. she was somewhere nearby. I couldn't see her. I tried to listen...

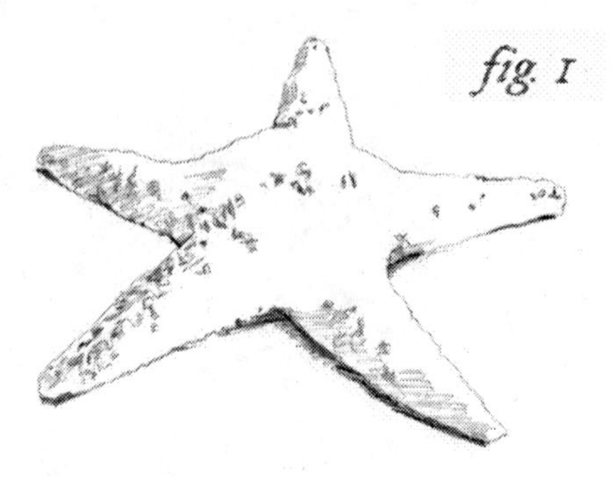

The plane took off and the first flight attendant, with the head flight attendant for reinforcement, brought the wife a sleeping pill to help her relax. They handed it to her like nurses, in a paper cup with another cup of water. They reassured her and the husband that there was such a thing as an air marshal. Like a police officer in the skies, the head flight attendant said, an FBI agent who does nothing but fly back and forth across the country on commercial jets and make sure no one takes over the plane. The wife nodded and swallowed the pill and the husband looked around for the air marshal. For two hours the husband did crossword puzzles out of a flimsy purple paperback with a brass Navy pen while his wife rested in her deep, drug-induced sleep. Then the dark-skinned man got up and started walking toward them. The girl watched him rise and felt the starfish grip her chest. She touched it and breathed, as she'd learned to, but it did not release. The husband sat up straight. He glanced at the man and at his sleeping wife and back at the man. He gripped his armrest hard with one hand, and the starfish gripped the girl harder as she watched the husband's other hand go white around his golden pen.

The squad car stops a few blocks past Trinity Church and the officer tells Martin to wait there. We're all waiting for something! Martin shouts as the officer jogs off. He watches the officer move off behind the squad car, and he notices two blocks back the empty lot, the hole with the cranes and lights, the fence with a continuous supply of fresh flowers sticking out of it. The officer jogs down the street towards the emptiness where the towers had been. I slept through the whole damn thing, Martin thinks. People were running everywhere. Those photographs of people covered in gray dust like ash—they marched up this very street. I was asleep in a dorm room. When they woke me up and said, A plane hit the World Trade Center, I pictured a seaplane like those on Lake Union in Seattle. I don't know why, it just made more sense. It was more believable for it to have been a small plane, for it to have been a mistake. Those people in the towers, those people marching up the street, what their dreams must be like.

fig. 3

Am I blind, Spivey? Just in the mind, maybe? I don't know. Surely reason hasn't left me entirely yet, has it? And I can see in the traditional sense, and that's something, I can see you, sitting across the table, and I can see S when she sits across a table, and that's an alleviation of loneliness, a different perspective on life like a drug could give, and that's what leads to happiness and what pulls people out of feeling like they're in hell; and so I don't think I am that man, sitting and listening to the television night after night. But I do feel guilty, like you said I would, and like I knew you would say, not just because I had nothing to do with the towers but because I'm in here, and even though I'm alone at night like everyone else I'm not LONELY because I can SEE the person across the table...you see? Even if, like you say, the blind man in my head isn't real, it doesn't mean there aren't people who really went blind when the planes exploded, or people who weren't just born blind. I'm sure there are people who deserve to see more than I deserve to see. People with kids. People with loves of their lives. People with people who love them, and depend on them saying "I love you"—and they depend on them right back, on being able to see that love in the other person's eyes that it's true and that it's something they both need. If you don't depend on that, if you don't need to see that, then you don't deserve the gift of sight as much as the person who went blind, and can't see that anymore, and can't give the person looking at them the same gift. There has to be a negative space there that a person can fill, and loneliness is that negative space with no potential, the empty hole, the blind man searching for the love of his life that he lost, right? So: Something About the Blind Man is just that blindness is another loneliness, another hell, another metaphor for death.

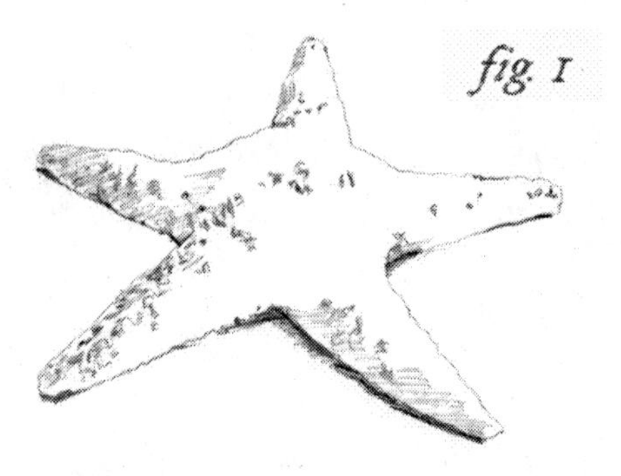

The girl with the starfish tattoo watched the husband's knuckles turn white as the man walked down the aisle. The man walking down the aisle pointed to the bathroom and said to the husband, with no accent, Just going to the bathroom. The man walking down the aisle was moving toward the husband and wife. He got closer and closer. He was almost there when the plane lurched, the girl dreamed, from turbulence, and the man with no accent and an expensive phone and dark skin and the makings of a thin beard and not-enough-luggage-to-actually-be-planning-on-ever-landing fell against the wife from the jolt of the plane. The girl with the starfish tattoo lost her breath from the force of the starfish's grip on her breast and the husband did exactly what any good and loyal American husband would do if a dark-skinned foreigner with a funny voice and expensive-looking clothes and a terrorist's glare walked down the aisle of a plane and tried anything funny: the husband clenched his golden pen in his hand and slammed it into the man's dark face, again and again, until the man fell on the carpet, crumpled and defeated, and, thank the Good Lord, out of sight.

They must dream of the fall, Martin thinks, looking up at the empty sky. Or of sitting in a cubicle and hearing someone yell, Oh my god! and turning and seeing a plane out the window. That's what they see. The ground rushing up, the plane rushing towards. In *No Exit,* Sartre imagines that in hell a person can stare off into space and put themselves back on earth and see what is happening without them. Martin wonders if any of those people are dead and doing just that, if they are staring at him. And if they are, what are they saying to the other people sitting with them in the stifling hot waiting room Sartre created? What are they saying about him? What would they tell him to do?

fig. 3

Here's something: hell is other people ONLY *if those people refuse to do something. If they refuse to do something, then it's like they've made you blind. Doing nothing give us nothing to see, nothing to love. And so I have a responsibility, Spivey. I must do something with my life. WE* ALL MUST DO SOMETHING.

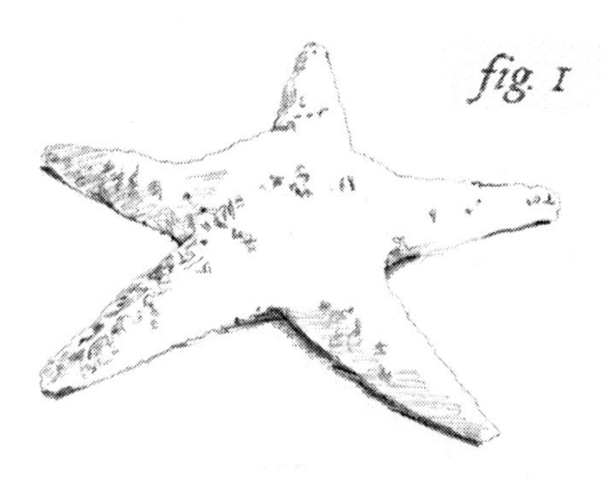

She heard the man scream, and heard other passengers scream, and then it was quiet for a long moment. The husband's hands were covered with blood and shaking when he finally broke the silence by yelling, Somebody do something! And the girl with the starfish tattoo climbed over the bloody husband and his fainted wife and said, It's okay, it's going to be okay, and she held out a hand to the man on the ground, the dark-skinned man who was pleading up to her, pleading without eyes, Please, I can't see anything. Please. Do something. Please, please. And she was looking at the man when she heard something far away, and felt something hit her shoulder, and that's when she woke up, someone was tapping her and saying, Miss? Miss? We're here. And the girl with the starfish tattoo saw a man she didn't recognize smiling next to her, and she turned to look out the window and saw that this man was right, they had landed and were moving slowly across the runway. I'm jealous, the man said. I've never been able to sleep through a flight, and the girl with the starfish tattoo looked back at him and nodded and rubbed her eyes. She tried to think. There was something she forgot to tell her brother, something she forgot to do, but she couldn't remember, and she assumed it wasn't important.

Martin coughs and looks down at the vomit at his feet. He looks up and sees that the sky is turning purple with the coming sun. He sees the flickering lights of a plane, too high to cause damage, high as it should be, heading to the airport. The voices, he thinks. The people sitting in a room and watching me. They're telling me to do something. Thousands of them singing, Do something do something do something.

fig. 3

But what do I do?

fig. 1

fig. 2

fig. 3

November 22, 2009

Something about H*appiness*

*Today a package arrived of forwarded mail from my apartment. Something from the Fifth Avenue's production company in Seattle. Somehow I'm still on all these publicists' mailing lists; I guess they don't realize I'm not going to be able to write about their new season. The galley said: "*H*appiness: a new play by Martin Patrick Simon." Folded inside the front of the paper cover was a one-sheet with biographical stuff and blurbs of good reviews about his past work in New York. There's a picture of the playwright, too. Looks to be in his late-20s. From Olympia originally, been in New York for a while, now coming back to the Northwest to be artistic director at the Fifth. The play though. I started reading it last night and finished this morning. It's all about happiness, (I expected that from the title, I guess) and given the playwright's late-twenties age it made sense that it would involve a sort of Sartreian existential search. So: the play starts with a sister picking her little brother up from work in Seattle. It's election day, the day Barack Obama was getting elected last year (a nice, sort of obvious-but-still-good setting). Characters: A boy named Patrick, 18, moved to*

Seattle from New Jersey to live with his older sister (Claire, 22) after their parents died in a car crash that summer. After the parents died they sold the house they grew up in and the boy put college on hold and so now the play starts and they're still trying to figure shit out, trying to figure out how to be happy in this new place. So BOOM, there's the crisis of conflict, stage one of the narrative cycle. That's followed by the actual conflict. The characters want to be happy, but what's the opposing force? Unhappiness! Yes, all that shit that happens and steals happiness from a person. That's all already happened of course, off stage (the parents died, drunken driver, etc, so there's the memory of that they have to deal with, the new lack of that familial love) and then there's the opposing force of reality (how is a person happy if they don't have a model of happiness to look to?) It comes out that mom and dad were never exactly the most loving parents—so their death wasn't just the death of LOVING PARENTS, but rather the death of ANY POSSIBILITY OF EVER BEING LOVED by parents. So now they're out there, in Seattle, Patrick and Claire, trying to find happiness. It's a simple premise, but it's set up just the way I would want it to be set up: two fragile characters standing at the edge of a great windy cliff, being pushed into the great unknown darkness by nothing violent, nothing evil, but just TIME and REALITY and SHIT. We're all forced into the future against our wills, aren't we Spivey? So: Act One takes place entirely in Claire's car. The boy works at a Starbucks in the U-District and the sister's place is in Greenlake so she picks him up on her way home sometimes (the whole thing's written very Seattle-specific). Act One begins and they're talking about their parents and the election, wondering what their parents would have thought of Obama, and it's fine because the parents were very liberal and it's all done in a very if-only-they-could-have-been-here-sort of way, but with a very real revolutionary undertone, and the conversation devolves into this incredibly sad and depressing mutual confusion between the siblings, like they just don't have any sort of guidance or any sort of love in their lives. It comes out that the sister had moved to Seattle for medical school, but when the parents died she deferred for a year and got a job writing pharmaceutical ad copy. The dialogue is full of 'beat' after 'beat' after 'beat' moments, so it's slow while reading it and you know there's just silence and whatever faint sound effect the director will put in, the driving whispery whoosh sound. It reads almost like Pinter but without the funny moments. It's going to depend, I think, a lot on how good the actors are, but the act ends with the sister starting to cry as they pull up to her building, and telling her brother she "was hoping she'd be happy today," because it's the election day, and there's a party tonight, and the brother starts to say something, and then doesn't, and then starts to again, and then doesn't, and then it's written that there's a sudden huge BANG noise (the playwright indicates it should be metal against metal, but also just yanking the sound plug out of its jack will probably make a significant enough squeal to shock the audience) and the lights go out completely, so that you think or realize or wonder if Patrick and Claire have just crashed into the building, and that's the end of Act One.

(Note: I really need to get a copy of this to S somehow. She would like it, or at least she would have interesting things to say about it. The Claire character is like that girl in that novel she loves so much and keeps asking me if I've read, even though I think she's given me two copies of it in the last year. It's good for someone alone, someone trying to be strong, trying to figure out how to hope, trying to figure out what optimism is supposed to look like. Not all that different than what we're coached to try and figure out in here...eh, Spivey?)

Dancing, dashing, darting, fluttering: I am a flitting white bird. I am a light, I am a star. I flicker like the white moon when glanced at through passing black trees. Once I was caught but now I am free. I am a light. Let me be a gleaming star to guide you.

Those were the opening lines of my professor's novel, the book that changed me from the girl I was to the woman I am. But it was in the third person, not like I wrote it here. *She* was a white bird, *she* had been caught and was now free. She would guide the reader. She was a light and a star.

This is not a coincidence, for now I am a light.

Now, I am a star.

It was never a coincidence.

This will be a horror story.

Three a.m. downstairs at an Irish pub on U street in the District of Columbia. The bartender is cleaning glasses and drinking a final pint with me. I'm drunk, my hair is in my face and I'm having trouble crossing my legs while keeping my balance on the barstool. He fills the pints again. On nights like this I drink Irish whiskey at whatever concert I have to review,

Guinness afterwards if I don't have to drive back to campus before morning. Tonight I've been at a show on 14th street and have come here after only because this bartender-friend lets me stay after close to listen to the jukebox and talk. I suppose it passes the time for him, to have someone to talk to while he closes, even a drunk, pretentious girl he knows only a little and only as an acquaintance through other people. He lives with a friend's ex-boyfriend and on nights like this they sometimes let me sleep and sober up on their couch. In the morning I'll take a cab back into the District to get my car, wherever I've left it, and then I'll drive back down I-95 into Virginia and to campus. Some girls would think this is strange but I don't care. And I haven't slept with either of the roommates because I don't care to.

One night it is three a.m. and the bartender closes the curtains and locks the door. We listen to the Smashing Pumpkins on the jukebox. He cleans pint glasses. I smoke Parliament cigarettes someone left in the bathroom. We talk about our nights, and then I slip off the stool and walk to the bathroom. I am walking and I realize I've crossed some new line of drunkenness. The room is a tilting watercolor of lights and stars surrounding me, gravity pushing me off balance. I know I am going to throw up. The bartender follows me to the bathroom, and I think he knows, too; I think he is going to come and hold my hair while I puke. He says: I just want to make sure you're okay. And for the moment I think, What a nice guy he is, really, what a kind gentleman, but just when I see the toilet and am about to bend over he grabs me. His fingernails cut the dry skin on my hips like talons, and puke flies out from the jolt of the grab, some in the toilet and some on the tile floor. His hand go down into my pants and force them down, still buttoned, tight and hurting. He turns me toward him so I can smell his breath. Guinness and smoke. He throws me on top of the sink. I'm sitting on its rim, and he shoves himself between my legs, my still buttoned jeans dangling around my ankles. I don't realize it. I don't realize what is happening until he is inside me. It stings, dry like a rope burn. He has to lick his fingers and rub himself to get it all the way in. I watch him lick his hand and wonder what he is doing. I see how skinny and white his legs are. I see how small and skinny he is. He doesn't try to kiss me, just moves back and forth, his hands clutching my hips. I want to be sick again—I can taste bitter acid, bile, building in my mouth. I ask him to stop so I can throw up. But then it doesn't matter, because I get sick out the other end. All the night's Guinness and falafel sprays onto the sink, a torch of liquid obsidian shit. He pulls himself out and I fall to the floor. He is huge and furious, staring down at me. You shit on my fucking cock! You fucking cunt shit! I try to climb up to the toilet but he pushes me down in the puke from before. I throw up next to the toilet again. I start to feel better. I start to see what's happened. Then he leaves the bathroom and I pull on my pants without my underwear and I try to think of how I can get out, where I can stay. I try to turn over but he returns. He has a bucket and is throwing water on me. Warm water, the mop water, or the bleach water from the sink they use to clean the glasses. I am on the floor, warmer from the water, staring at my panties hanging from his shoe, stained and ripped. He yells and kicks. I try to cover myself. I look at the ceiling. I see what's happening. The lights are hot and white. I see what's happening.

I see what's happening.

The bartender left and I stayed on the floor for I don't know how long. I woke later under the hot white fluorescent lights of the bathroom. Someone found me, the next day's bartender, I don't remember. I sat in a police car with a blanket on a bright morning. They actually give you blankets, I thought, like on TV, and I thought how I had actually been raped; that this was my new reality. *Rape victim. Sexual assault victim*. I heard a police officer say to someone outside: I hate these calls, I just hate them. Later, in police reports and legal papers, I would be referred to as The Victim. Something awful had been done to me, and people hate having to know about the awful things that can be done to people. But that night I came closer to becoming the woman of my professor's novel.

I'd read the novel before the night in the bathroom, but not like I read it all the nights after. I felt a kinship with the woman who was a light, who was a star. The woman was not raped in my professor's story, but she was the product of one. She was a young woman at the start of the book, 22 years old, like me. The plot was like that of the old movie *Chinatown*; but instead of John Huston as the master patriarch it was a black senator from Virginia; and instead of Faye Dunaway as his obedient daughter it was a slave-daughter the senator kept in a run-down motel. The apartment was set in the same town where I first read the novel. In Williamsburg, Virginia, where I went to college.

Ignorant of any family and convinced she was an orphan, my professor's protagonist knew her father only as a gracious foster parent. She would bathe with him in the motel room tub and kiss his penis as it rose above the bubbles. She knew nothing else; her motel room was Plato's cave and her father was a gruesome shadow bearing down. It was an allegory of slavery and racial persecution. That this took place in Williamsburg, site of Colonial Williamsburg, was not a coincidence. Williamsburg is an entire town built on the concept that the past can exist in constant recreation, can evolve into a more perfect image of history. Can change, not history, but how we remember it, our perception of the past. The tourists arrive to see what life was like for the founders of this nation, not caring that what they're seeing is nothing but life-sized historical fiction. How could they know the difference?

This is where I had come from the night I was raped, and what I went back to the following day. This is not a coincidence.

He didn't kill me: it could have been worse. It could have been someone I couldn't identify, and he might not have gotten caught. I didn't bleed—that was good. There was no blood at all. Not even on my hips where his claws dug in. Still, I wanted to kill him. To see him powerless, the heel of my boot against his neck, crushing his trachea. But he was taken away to courtrooms and I was taken home to Chicago and to hospitals. Later I would move here to North Carolina, to Asheville, and get a job as a waitress. I thought I would stop drinking after it happened but I only drink more now. And writing this, sitting in the dark and thinking of my professor's book and what happened, I sip whiskey to wash out the remembered smell and taste. Whiskey is the sweet, unspoiled caramel of the life before.

It's towards the middle of my professor's book that the

slave girl is saved from the motel by free siblings who find out about her after going through their father's finances after he is hospitalized for a mild heart attack. She goes on to become a writer. It's all she can do, she explains. She wants people to understand that she felt loved during it all, that life is all about how you look at it. She talks about Plato's cave, and the comfort of shadows. She didn't know that the life she was living was horrible. She didn't know that she wasn't free. She had felt loved by her father, the one who kept her there, and when he died in the hospital, she went to the hospital and wept at his bedside, where his other children refused to be. As a free woman, life was different. What she had thought was love turned out to be terror. And now that she was free of that terror, all she felt was fear, fear that she would never love again.

I couldn't help but want to write, and I asked one of the psychologists in Chicago why she, the doctor, thought that was. I didn't understand it, I said. I don't understand why I want to write, I just do. I don't understand why the slave girl in the novel says there is nothing else she can do. Because there is nothing else *I* can do either.

It's because she wants to take control, the doctor told me. I see why you identify with her, she said. When someone writes something, when *you* write something, you're creating this other world where you are in complete control. And that's what I think the girl in the novel was saying, why she said she couldn't do anything else. She'd never had any control at all. You want to be a writer because you know, on some level, it will give you control over what's happening. But I think you write about music because you're writing about your own life, reporting on something that actually happened to you. It seems to me that you don't want to create a new life, it's more that you want the life you've lived to be different. And I wonder if you don't take advantage sometimes. Sometimes I even wonder if you're telling me the truth about what happened that night in the bar. Sometimes when you tell it, you're wearing pants. Sometimes a skirt.

I live in Asheville now, a city in the western hills of North Carolina. It's a place populated by those who were born here, and those who came for the pottery and the trees that change color at sunset. The day I arrived I was sitting in a tattoo parlor on Biltmore Avenue and I asked the gray-haired tattoo artist where he was from. He was inking in a blue starfish on my chest and kept working as he talked. The needle made its whirring noise. Came from Raleigh, he said. Friend of mine moved out here first, told me Asheville was built on a big fucking crystal, just under the dirt and trees. So I says to him, I gotta fuckin see that. And so I came, married 'is sister, and I still ain't never left.

He sat back from the tattooed starfish and looked me in the eyes, smiled. The old man was a professional; he didn't stare at my exposed breasts. You want a smoke? he asked. Thanks, I said, and he handed me a hand-rolled cigarette from a pack at his feet. I added: Thanks for not looking, too, by the way, and he chuckled. I'm an artist, kiddo. He dug in his brown rucksack for a lighter. If I want a see a naked lady I go home and tell my wife I'm takin her to Tahiti. The clothes'll just fall off.

My professor told me her novel was based on her own life—but that she had never been involved in incest. She told me that writers realize, with time, that in order for others to understand what they've gone through they can't tell it exactly the way it happened—they have to embellish. That's what fiction is: reality tilted in such a way that the reader can see the truths of the world more clearly. It's like what the psychologist said about not believing me—I'm not even sure if I remember everything exactly the way it happened that night any more, but I do remember the truth of what happened to me. And after what happened I didn't want to just write about music anymore. I wanted to be a light, to be a star, to illuminate truths about surviving in this world.

My mom and step-dad flew in from Chicago after it happened. They came and got me and my graduation got put on hold. I went home, back to the room I slept in as a child. I went to counseling twice a week somewhere near the Northwestern campus. Whether it was a part of the hospital or medical school there, I don't remember. One of the doctors told my mom that my case was fairly typical. Then my mom repeated that to me. She told me that that was good, that I had had a fairly typical rape experience. It was usually someone the victim knew in some capacity. Drugs or alcohol were usually involved. My mom told me to thank God it hadn't been worse. My step-dad told me the same.

The doctors put me on antidepressants and sleep medication. In the waiting room I looked around at all the other girls sitting there waiting. We studied each other, wondering why we were there. At first I thought that what I'd gone through was special. But I listened to what the girls said at a group session, not allowed to talk to them, and except for details we'd all been through basically the same thing—not just rape or assault, but the rest of it too. We were all typical cases, all trying to figure out what we were supposed to be doing now, especially now.

I had thought that because of what I had been through I would look at the world in a unique way, like the protagonist in the novel. It was a horrible realization, a nightmare, to know we'd all gone through the same thing. And so one night I was lying in bed listening to Leonard Cohen and staring at the bookshelf and thinking how even these great writers, these Brontes, these Woolfs, these Miltons and Shakespeares, in the end they're just another spine in a long, ever-growing row of spines, like a sea snake that never dies, but just gets longer and longer until it circles the world and begins to eat its own tail, and the history of world's literature repeats itself in a massive uroboros. I took a handful of the sleeping pills and slugged them down. Then I snuck downstairs and found a bottle of wine my parents had left out after dinner. They had been drinking a lot now that I was back. I heard my step-brother Eddie watching TV in the living room and crept back to my bedroom. I said a prayer and asked God to look after Eddie and my parents, meaning it. Then I sucked down what was left in the bottle, walked to the hamper and threw the bottle in it, and then I lay down on the bed to wait and see if I would feel any different.

I woke on the tile bathroom floor, covered in purple vomit. At first I thought I was back there, in the bar, but it was *Eddie* who was over me now, shouting for me to wake up.

They took me to the hospital. My sixteen-year-old step-brother had come to my room looking for cigarettes and saw the empty bottle of pills. He tried to wake me up. When he couldn't he screamed for his dad and they carried me to the bathroom and his dad stuck a finger down my throat.

I tried to convince them that I wasn't trying to kill myself, that I was only trying to feel something. I told them how this new depression was like a *thing* I was just trying to understand. But it's not something easy to explain, I said, searching for words. I wanted to say that I was just trying to feel like I was feeling. But to say I was just trying to feel like I was feeling? It sounds so unaware, so naïve and uncertain. But it's that uncertainty that I was trying to explain in the first place, that desire to sink to the very sea floor of depression, toward those sea creature cousins of Grendel that only appear when I'm furthest from the surface, when I've gotten as deep into the *thing* as I can, trying to understand this *thing* that's a part of me, that's maybe the *real* me, the light that I'm supposed to become, the star that I'm supposed to grow into—but it's then, when I've come closest to understanding this *thing*, it's then that they give me these pills that are like buoyancy capsules, keeping me afloat and as far away from the truth about the *thing*—the truth about *me*!—as possible.

They put me in a hospital for a few weeks anyway, where just like the waiting room I was surrounded by people just like me, all of us dressed in the same white pajamas like drunk and crazy angels. I told my story and it was about on par with the others, both the first part at the bar and the second part at home. One girl, though, a teenager named Jesse with cropped hair and burn scars covering one half of her face, told this story. As far as I know she'd been in the hospital for over a year, and she told this story every time we had group meetings. I never got tired of it:

When I was, like, fifteen or whatever, I don't even remember any more, my dad, he, he was an asshole. A fuckin asshole, man. Vietnam fucked him up somethin terrible. Was just me 'n him. Moms died when I was twelve or thirteen. Fuckin drunk driver, man. My dad, he made me stay home from school after that, keep the house in shape durin the day. He'd work sober then come home late bombed to fuck and gone and want me to cook somethin for him. Beat the shit out of me, too. Talk about how I was a pussy like my mother and never woulda made it in no war like he did. He liked to talk about how many kids he killed just like me, little pussy girls like me just for lookin at 'im wrong, and how if I hadn't-a been 'is own kid, and if he wouldn't-a gotten killed for it, he'd just as soon be done with me too. How I was too ugly to hug, but he'd still come into my room somes times and grab me and fuck me. So after like two years of this the old man passes out watchin the TV and I'm up still doin my home school shit cuz if it aint done in the morning when he leaves for work I'll catch hell, and there's this whole thing on 'Nam on. This documentary thing, I don't know. And they's showing these monks in Saigon, showin them pouring gasoline on each other and lighting themselves on fire to protest the war. And I think I'm gonna show this bastard something, that he can't keep me no fuckin slave. And so I goes outside and I gets the lantern his daddy gave him and I shake it and can hear the kerosene in there sloshing 'round, and so I sets myself down on the living room floor and pour it all over me and get a match ready. I throw the lantern at him and shout, I'll see you in Hell bastard! and I light the match. There's this loud fucking Whoosh noise and I smell burning hair and everything goes black. Next thing I know my whole body stings like it fell asleep, y'know, like how a leg'll fall asleep? It was like that, all over. Everywhere. So I realize I'm tied to a hospital bed and can't fuckin move nothin, not even my eyes. Nurse comes in a little bit later, and she whispers to me—Sweetie, she calls me—she whispers how the old man, how he must have passed out from the smoke. He was dead. But I was closer to the door. She tells me how this neighbor couple happened to be drivin by right when I lit the match and that whoosh lit up the living room like a fuckin rocket. And, well, them neighbors got me out, all covered in third degree burns and missin half my face, but they got me out. Couldn't get to the old man where he was, all that gas I spilled on the carpet. I'm glad they couldn't get to 'im, even if I'm stuck here. I'm glad they let the old man burn. May he light up fuckin Hell.

No one said it, but everyone in the circle was jealous of that story.

I was able to finish my degree in Chicago, so I didn't have to go back to Virginia. I satisfied the few credits I still needed to graduate through some online courses and that was that. I don't think my parents would have let me go back to Virginia anyways. I moved down to Asheville, not because I'd heard it was built on a big fucking crystal like the tattoo artist had, but because I had driven through the town once my junior year and always wanted to go back. It seemed to be a good place to make a fresh start. My parents were apprehensive but they let me take the car and my prescriptions and the numbers of some psychologists at Duke and I left.

The week before I left Chicago, we all went to the aquarium. We were going to have my goodbye dinner downtown and it seemed like something fun the family could do beforehand. I loved the aquarium when I was a little girl. More even, I think, than I later loved music and books. When I was little I would run around yelling to my parents to hurry up so I could touch the sponges and starfish at the big open tank they had for that purpose. In my 5th grade yearbook, in a blank space beneath my picture where everyone had to write what they wanted to be when they grew up, I wrote: "Marine Biologist (ocean doctor)." Three years in a row for Halloween I was Ariel from the *Little Mermaid*.

I'd have dreams that I lived under the sea with the under-the-sea creatures, complete with the Disney musical score. This time, my first time to any aquarium in years, I wandered slowly away from the rest of them in the blue-lit underground tunnels, the black carpeted hallways. My mom had been worried that I'd be nervous, to be in the dark like that. Are you sure you want to go to the aquarium? she's asked, her voice all concern. Everyone assumed the bar was dark where I'd been attacked, but they didn't know how bright it had been in that bathroom, the buzzing fluorescent bulbs. This underwater blue was so peaceful and warm, like stage lights during the quiet bridge of a beautiful song—when the guitars sink and the keyboards rise and the drummer slows and wipes his brow. I love that moment, when everything calms from whatever distorted catharsis the verses contain and the world can just stop. Blue lights on a singer, all ears reaching for the words—it's like the whole world changes.

I wandered through the aquarium tunnels looking for the tank that held the starfish and anemones. It was still there, but looked smaller than it had when I was little. There was a group of children surrounding it, reaching in and touching the creatures, a field trip from school. A woman teacher not much older than me was talking to them. One of the little boys, he must have been 10 or 11, held up a starfish that was missing one of its points, an arm or leg. What's wrong with this one? he asked. Is it retarded or something? All the boys snickered. The teacher shushed him and said, No, it's just hurt. Starfish can lose a piece of them like that, but they grow it back. Like how Mr. Gonzales' iguana lost its tail and it grew back? Remember?

The children nodded and the boy tossed the legless

starfish back into the tank. The group moved on. Alone, I looked into the shallow water at the starfish the boy had held up. I reached in to hold it, but it had reattached itself hard to the rocks, and I couldn't pry it loose. I tried harder but it was holding fast. I started to cry, trying to pull the starfish off the rocks, and Eddie came and found me, and we all went to dinner. We shouldn't have let you wander alone in the dark, my mom said.

Ten days later, on the day I arrived in Asheville, I checked into the hotel where I was planning to live for awhile and went in search of the tattoo parlor. I met the man who was too much of a gentleman to look at my breasts. He told me how Asheville was built on a big fucking crystal, and I have a tattoo of a blue starfish under my left breast now. It covers where the bartender's foot broke three of my ribs. All the starfish's points are intact.

That was almost three years ago now, and I've gotten used to seeing the starfish there on my chest when I shower and dress. At first I was conscious of it all the time, it was almost like I could feel it, gripping me. But that gradually faded. I worry sometimes of what it will be like next time I sleep with someone. I worry what I will say when he asks about the tattoo. But while there have been men I've wanted to show it to, I haven't for any of them.

There was one night, a few years ago, when I felt the clutch more than I ever did. The Smashing Pumpkins had come to Asheville to play nine nights at the Orange Peel, and on the night of the first show something happened that made me feel it more even than when it was getting inked with the whirring needle, more even than when I had lain on the bathroom floor in a skirt or pants getting kicked. Just the idea of seeing the Smashing Pumpkins in a club as small as the Orange Peel made me feel something between ultimate excitement and ultimate terror, it made my heart beat hard beneath the tattoo.

They were from Chicago, and it was the Smashing Pumpkins that I listened to all through high school. It was the Smashing Pumpkins that I listened to when I first made out with a boy. It was them when I left for college, and them when I found out my grandmother had passed away in her sleep. The night I drank the wine and took the pills I was listening to the Smashing Pumpkins. And as I walked to the restroom that night at the bar it was the Smashing Pumpkins playing on the jukebox; Billy Corgan's nasally voice was everywhere, "Today is the greatest day I've ever known," and the bartender made the decision to do what he did, and he followed me.

The night of the concert I got out of the shower and looked at myself naked in the foggy mirror. I was so nervous. I wiped my hand across the mirror and stared at the blue starfish clutching my chest. I recited those lines from my professor's novel: *I was caught but now am free. I will be light. I will be a gleaming star.*

That I remembered them in the wrong tense is not a coincidence.

I will be a light, I will be a gleaming star, I said. I was writing a feature for the *Chicago Reader* about the concert. It was my first cover story with them. It was an opportunity, the editor said, *To show us what you can do.*

I drove the three miles from my apartment to the club with the windows down, smelling the trees, thinking how much more beautiful trees are at night when the headlights of a car glance over them briefly, so there's just the suggestion of the tree, the scattered branches and shadows interplaying like flames in a black and white television explosion.

After the concert, I remember I stumbled outside hoping to run into the band. I remember I was drunk and opened a second pack of cigarettes. I remember that I couldn't remember where I'd parked but I wasn't in any shape to drive home yet anyway. I remember my t-shirt was dripping with sweat from the heat inside the club. I remember my armpits itched and my bra felt heavy. I remember thinking that, even though the band didn't do interviews, I would wait and talk to them. I remember telling myself that I could write a good story.

A dozen or so others were waiting around the backstage door too, with a couple security guards in yellow and black shirts to make sure we didn't get out of hand. I leaned against the brick wall and tried to light a cigarette. A stray hair got caught in the flame and singed quickly. I laughed and imagined what people would have thought if my head had suddenly burst into flames. I hiccupped and tasted whiskey and burnt hair. I remember I had been so drunk inside. I remember I had to plug my ears when Billy sang "Today is the greatest day." I remember I hiccupped again and tasted vomit. I leaned against the brick wall, and I remember that it was wet from water or from someone's piss, and I remember not caring which.

I remember there had been this guy in the club, this skinny white asshole with a long mop of natural dreadlocks hanging down to his waist like an old burlap sac. During the first song he bumped into me and made me spill my plastic cup of whiskey. It had seemed intentional because he apologized so fast and sarcastically that it was like he'd expected it to happen, and then he tried to wipe my shirt off like he was helping, tried to pretend he wasn't trying to feel me up. I remember his hair reeked of pot and incense. I shoved him and he laughed. I moved away, tried to watch the concert. Then I remember I saw him again, a few songs later, when I was back at the bar. There were people I knew from my day job at the restaurant there. I went up to them, but none of them seemed to know this guy. I remember someone said that a lot of people had come from out of town for the shows.

The dreadlocked guy kept trying to get close to me. Kept asking if he could buy me a replacement beer. When he saw me taking notes of the set list he asked what I was doing. Was I that big of a fan or was I reporter or something? I remember I shoved away from him again and that was the last time I saw him inside. But I've thought about it a lot since then. I have tried to remember everything exactly as it happened. Now that I am writing this I remember I did see him again. I remember everything that happened, how I let myself get as drunk as I did before, how I said to that girl in the mirror, Let what will come, come. When people from Chicago or Williamsburg ask me how I'm doing now, how I'm getting on in Asheville, or when my professor writes to ask how the writing is going—then I tell them this story of what I remember.

I tell them,

This will be a horror story.

I'm leaning against the brick wall and I see him come walking down the street towards me. There were people from my job at the show, but they already left. I am waiting to see if I can talk to the band. I don't know anyone here. My breath tightens as the guy and his ugly mass of hair approach. I feel the starfish getting hot and squeezing my chest with a sharp grip. He walks right up to me. "Hey babe," he says.

"Get the fuck away," I say. He smiles and points at the beer stain on my t-shirt. "Sorry again, about the beer," he says. I hate his smell of sweat and hemp. "Fuck off," I say again, and he stops smiling and stands there off balance. He looks angry. Some other people waiting for the band look over at us. A security guard in his black and yellow shirt, wearing a huge black cowboy hat starts walking towards us. The guy with the hair starts yelling. "What the fuck's your problem? I'm just trying to be nice, to apologize, and you're being this fucking loudmouth bitch about it! Well fuck you, you fucking cunt!" His face is within six inches of my face when he yells these last words. He hits the brick wall over my shoulder. His fist lands near my head, to scare me. And I spit a smoky mouthful of phlegm in his eyes. He steps back, puts a hand to his face. He makes like he's going to punch me and the starfish squeezes hard over my speeding heart. It grows hot, grows larger, clutches me tighter. It is burning and I wait for him to hit me. But the security guard is there. "On your way, Dreads," the guard says. He is gripping the sweaty dreadlocked guy hard by the hair. "Just get the fuck away, understand? You got a ride home?" The guy struggles to get out of the guard's grip, grunting and bent over. He trips and falls, but the guard keeps hold. The hair is like a pile of rope he could strangle me with. "Yeah I gotta fucking ride!" he screams, "Leggo my fuckin hair!" The security guard lets go and pushes him out into the street. We watch him walk back up the hill toward the front of the club, wrapping his dreadlocks in a large square knot behind his head. He turns from the top of the hill. "Sorry about the beer, bitch!" he yells back, showing us his middle finger. Everyone waiting by the stage door looks at him, then at me. I just look down and try to relax. I rub the starfish on my chest, can feel my heart slowing beneath it. Everything is hot, I'm burning up. "You okay?" The guard takes off the cowboy hat and turns toward me. He runs a hand across his bald head. "Yeah, thanks," I whisper. "Listen," he says, "I think we need to let Dreads walk up that fuckin way and you walk

that fuckin way, and we just leave each other alone, got it? You got a ride home?" I lie: "I'm meeting some friends at a restaurant." "Alright then," he says, and turns back to the other security guards. I catch my breath and start walking down the hill, in the opposite direction that Dreads walked. It's true I was invited for drinks at the restaurant but I'm drunk enough already and don't want to go. Dreads scared me, and I just want to go home. I could barely breathe when he was that close to me, when he punched the wall. Three years since the night in the bar. Still I can barely breathe.

If I were a real writer, I think, if I were a real writer and not just a music journalist, but a real writer, I could have total control. I could make the character version of myself be exactly the kind of person I want to be. That's the control I want. That slave girl in the book killed herself. So did her senator father after hearing the news. My professor, her sister had committed suicide. Maybe that's where the story comes from, but I have no way of knowing. All I know is that when we lose control of our lives, when we have lost all control (and even just the illusion of control), there really is no point in going on. Religion teaches us to give up control to a god. Christianity, Eastern religions, they all say the same thing, to give up our control to a higher power, to abandon our attachments to this world. But that Jesse girl at the hospital, some god gave her a drunk father who beat her, who raped her.

I get to my car but am still too drunk to drive it. I've parked further up Biltmore Avenue past the club, where not so many people driving to the show would think to park. The street up here is cobblestoned and lined with shops and offices of city officials, closed delis. My restaurant is on the other side of town, closer to the club. That's where most people would park. Gas lamps light the sidewalks and benches line the road, facing a few parallel-parked cars. A group of people walk past while I sit on one of the benches and wait for my body to metabolize a little more alcohol before driving the three miles home. They are chat-

ting about the show, to each other and to friends on cell phones. I sit on the bench and sigh. I light another cigarette. I close my eyes and wake in the middle of the night to the moon high in the sky and Dreads leaning over me. He holds my wrists down and traps me on the bench. He is laughing and spitting in my face again and again. "How do you like it?" he keeps whispering. "How do you like it?" His hair covers my face with its stink and I stare through it to the gas lamp flickering overhead. I try to breathe through his hair and he keeps spitting, squeezing my wrists. I pray for someone to see us; I see what's happening: I whisper that he can go fuck himself. He punches me in the face, on the cheekbone below my left eye. The back of my head hits the bench and the world spins, the gas lamps blur with the moon and we are surrounded in a universe of lights and stars. He stands and starts to unzip his pants. We are floating on a bench through a galaxy of lights, and I see what's happening: I kick my boot up with all my might, right between his skinny legs, and it is like something from a movie when he grabs his stomach and doubles-over onto his knees.

I float off the bench and grab his hair with hands not my own. I pull it hard like the security guard had. It had seemed like rope before, and it feels like rope as he is kneeling before me, and I am wrapping it around the handle of the bench and tying it as tight as I can. The lights gleam brighter, comets pass, asteroids fall, explosions surround us. I step on his back with all my weight and he struggles. I am all light, radiating, and I see my reflection in a gleaming star. There are certain species of starfish that can lose an arm, and not only will they grow it back but from the damaged arm a new starfish will grow. In the light I see the girl doing this, and I see what is happening, the woman I am becoming, and I see what will happen. Dreads is screaming and trying to get free, but the bench is bolted to the ground. You are the illumination of the earth, I say to the girl in the star, the girl being set free. We say together: You control the lights, You control the stars. You are a starfish. This is not a coincidence.

Dreads is still calling me a cunt when I watch myself take a lighter from a pocket and hold it to his greasy, rope-like hair. There is the flick, the spark, the smell, the WHOOSH! sound, a scream. Mostly, there is light. I am a light. A light. Alight.

It is dawn when Denis is forced up the hill. Rain dark and gray, like needles falling. Denis trips, coughs in the mud. His wrists tangle and rip in the sharp rope behind his back. He is dragged by the rope up to the top of the small mountain, is made to kneel in black mud and gravel, his cheek fallen and bruised against the smoothness of a wet, white stone.

Mud dripping from captors' boots; mud in his face and eyes. His knees dig into the mountain, slicing open, pink. A kick in the small of his back from one of his captors. A boot presses his face harder into the stone. Retching and heaving, he prays. Jesus, give me strength to forgive, he prays. Give me Your spirit, he prays. And then in the flash of a blade – I want to let go, Lord –he breathes air and rain, forgives. A blinking head tumbles off the edge of the stone. Blood seeps purple over the white stone and into the mountain. The man with the blade stops the rolling head with the heel of his boot.

Some time later two splashes ripple the Seine. The Christians come out from their dark places and retrieve the holy head and holy body of Denis, their martyr on the mountain, in the year of Our Lord 258.

This is the dream Martin has. He fell asleep reading.

The axe falls through the flesh of his neck and clangs against the white stone below, sparking, ringing as a bell. A flash of light and sound of metal and Denis is dead. Martin's book lies on the wood floor next to the tangled power strip beneath his desk. A book from his Catholic grandmother's shelf, the "true" stories of saints, of martyrs, the fodder for last night's dreams. He fell asleep watching a movie, trying to forget the stories he was reading, and the confused pang of jealousy he felt toward the characters.

He rises this Sunday morning into thoughts of his grandfather, buried three days ago in Olympia, and into thoughts on the possibility that after this there is simply nothingness, not Heaven or Hell, no consciousness at all. All weekend he's tried not to think about death. It seems even Hell would be preferable to a simple ending of existence. Perhaps that is Hell, he thinks. But it's hard to get his head wrapped around that idea.

Back home everyone said they were *so* happy to see him doing *so* well in New York. They are being polite—what else can they tell him? Martin's parents died in a car crash when he was a toddler, and he was raised by his grandparents until he left for college. In the eyes of his extended family he's never been seen as much more than the little boy who always got the most Christmas presents and attention at birthdays, he knows this. There was this moment: he and an aged version of a neighbor lady from his childhood found themselves sneaking into the liquor cabinet at the same time to spike their orange juice on the morning of the funeral. *We're all so proud of you, you and your plays,* she said him, the edge of the vodka bottle clinking against her glass, her voice seeming to him a mix of sarcasm and cynicism. They all resent him for leaving. His young cousins, the ones that became construction workers and car salesmen. No one else has moved away. They were all there when his grandfather died. A grand erasing ceremony, as Martin imagines it, all of them encircling the deathbed, praying Hail Marys like some terrible production of *Lear* where his grandfather shakes in bed with his tremors, wondering what the hell is going on, wondering what happened to his crown. Then, later, Martin's grandfather lying naked in a funeral home basement on an aluminum table, like a bit character in a television show. And, even still later, dressed in a new suit, in an immaculate coffin of red silk and oak, lowered into a concrete block surrounded by stone and earth, capped with fresh sod and a polished headstone bearing Martin's name, Martin Patrick Simon.

Some numbers click on a dial and he's looking at his own tomb. At what point does one die from cardiac arrest if they're buried alive? They can't all suffocate—the fear would be too intense. Plato's Cave. Ishmael going to sea. Is the world hotter or colder when you're buried beneath six feet of earth? Standing over the grave at the service, looking around at his family, Martin thought, This is my blood, these people here, that body down there, my parents just a short drive away in a different cemetery. The great aunt I never met is mixing with the dirt beneath that headstone over there, Aunt Joanne. We used her recipe for potatoes last night. The woman called Joanne has left her carbon-based body and now inhabits a carbohydrate-rich side dish. We distract ourselves with the stage directions in order to forget the final scene.

He remembers the weight of the coffin in his hands. A heaviness he had not expected, a heaviness that made it easy to let the coffin fall onto the machine that would guide it into the hole.

The plane landed at LaGuardia last night before nine and he was back to the Upper East Side by quarter of ten. He worked, sitting at the computer, writing until after four and drinking the scotch and smoking the cigarettes he bought last week after getting the call from his uncle. He typed furiously next to the unpacked suitcase thrown on the unmade bed, gibberish words on the screen, his eyes watery from smoke, the deadline already past for a draft of his new, untitled play. Something set in Seattle, he's been thinking. Something about happiness. But that's as far as he's really gotten.

Unable to sleep, he read some of the book on saints. *This may help you cope*, his grandmother had said, *help you understand that love continues on after we die.* They both knew she wanted it to seem like she was talking about his grandfather when she was really talking about Claire. Martin's grandmother had loved Claire. He had loved Claire. He'd asked Claire to marry him and she'd said yes without hesitating. Claire had been pretty and sweet. She had seemed smarter than Martin, which his grandmother had felt was a good thing, since he'd always been treated special and now needed someone to keep him grounded. Claire had represented Martin's future—a future of Catholic great-grandchildren and responsible financial living. Claire had meant Martin's grandmother didn't have to worry about Martin anymore; he would be taken care of after she was gone. She was frightened for him, living in New York, away from what family he had.

At the cemetery, his grandmother's grip on his arm was sharp and shaky; she dug her nails into his wrist as if losing her grip would result in her falling into the plot alongside her husband, in the place already paid for, beneath a stone already engraved with her name, too. She let go only after he'd helped her into the car and she'd clutched onto the somewhat drunk neighbor sitting beside her in back. That night, when she handed Martin the book on saints, she grabbed his wrist again. He wanted to tell her that he hadn't left Claire, she'd left him. He wanted to tell her about Claire and her photographer, Claire's confession. He wanted to tell her he hated Claire now, that any love he'd had for her now necessitated a hate, that it was a necessary dualism, like Good and Evil.

He gave up the writing and read some of the book of saints, but the stories of third-century decapitations were too much to take. He kept thinking of himself with his face in the mud, of his grandfather buried beneath six feet of dirt, of what it will be like when he dies. Putting the book aside, he inserted a DVD of *Annie Hall* into his computer and fell asleep at the lobster scene.

Sunday afternoon. Martin walks the sidewalks of 92nd street between First and Second Avenues, five-storey brick walk-ups lining his path. Heading east, the sun draws long tree-shadows that stretch ahead, parallel to the elongated ten-foot version of himself keeping stride. Walking with uncertain direction: to the bank, definitely, and then maybe a late breakfast, coffee and Tabasco eggs at the diner on Second. Or maybe just coffee and a cigarette on a bench overlooking the East River, searching for that optimism people associate with being near large bodies of water--that and the comfortable isolation of enjoying a coffee and a cigarette while healthier persons jog past. People improving themselves, keeping their bodies alive longer, releasing endorphins, struggling to stay chemically balanced. Claire used to jog, and he used to love that she jogged. He used to believe in God, too; going to church with his grandparents as a child he liked to believe his parents were hiding in the tabernacle, watching him, protecting him. Later he stopped believing. He realized he hated God for making it rain that particular day and taking them, just as he later would hate Claire for saying she was jogging while she was actually fucking some photographer and taking his idea of a fiancée away. A person cannot believe in a God-Who-is-Love, he thought, when love is proven so mortal.

For the months between Claire's confession and his grandfather's death, Martin focused exclusively on work, on getting a new play done while also working on this new Seattle-happiness thing, which didn't seem to be going anywhere anyway. He started drinking more and smoking again. More of both, more than ever, something his friends and colleagues have encouraged. *You deserve it*, they say. *Go out, party. Have a few. Forget the cunt.*

Approaching the corner of First Avenue, Martin sees an old black man in a Yankees sweatshirt and bulky headphones sitting on a low brick wall against the side of a Citibank vestibule. The man waves to Martin, and Martin gets ready to mutter 'Sorry, man'—he's heard every homeless-beggar plea worth hearing, from mothers of babies with HIV needing a special kind of milk that costs eighteen dollars a can, a man on 89th Street who follows you around singing Otis Redding until you pay him to stop. But he has nowhere to be and knows for a fact that he has a one-dollar bill in his front right pocket. He needs this distraction today, this other's life, to make himself feel better.

The man sticks out a thick hand and they shake.

Mornin', son, the man says.

Good morning. Martin nods and feels in his pocket for the dollar, but the man only sighs, doesn't ask for anything.

I was just settin here listnen to my music, he says, Just settin here praisen the Good Lord for this beautifo day here.

His head turns lizard-like side to side, looking up and down the sidewalk and seemingly everywhere but at Martin. His legs swing like cuts of meat off the brick wall.

Yeah, it's nice, Martin agrees. The whites of the man's eyes are stained with age, the pupils imperfect circles.

See son, the man says, wagging a finger in Martin's direction but still looking up and down 92nd street. I just got outta prison. I done sumptin I aint proud of, but I went and did my time, and the thing with jail—he coughs—the thing with jail...well, you hear what I'm sayin. You hear what I'm saying, right? Even the free man aint ever free. Not until the Good Lord come into 'is 'eart. I aint homeless or nuthin, I got a place to live. See, the Lord provided for me, gave me a place. Before, I was just like this.

He waves his arm to indicate the masses. A man jogging. A Puerto Rican woman with a white toddler strapped to her breast. A teenage mop-topped boy on a skateboard.

I was just like this. Goin to work, feedin my brother's kids, jus lookin forward to the weekend and the drink and bit of weed I'd take after work. See I did electrics. I wired the Domino sugar factory long time ago, and now they're tearing that stuff down. You know what it's like to have your life's work torn down?

Martin watches the jogger disappear down First Avenue. Dark hair, defined shoulders. Expensive running gear. Martin's sure he saw him not thirty minutes ago from his apartment when he'd woken unhappily to the sight of dust floating in the red sunlight like so many angry Queen Mabs before his thin red curtains. He'd pushed the curtains aside and watched this man and a woman jog side by side up the hill on 91st street toward Third Avenue. He sat on the edge of his bed and watched. Now the same man—hardly sweating at all—is jogging down the sidewalk away from him. Where's the woman? Had they really been together, or a pure coincidence of time and speed? Was Claire fated to meet the photographer? Was Martin fated to fall in love and then, later, out? His parents—were they fated to die early?

A dehydration hangover. How much did he drink last night?

Martin lights a cigarette. He expects to be chastised for smoking when the man looks him in the eye and points a finger. The man starts speaking, in a storyteller's voice, a grandfatherly, intimate tenor. See son, he intones, looking at Martin now with those stained eyes snug in their aged leather sockets. You see, in prison they give a man a chance to go to the church. So I went, went to see what all the fuss was about. Never went when I was a kid and never went when I wasn't a kid neither. So I go, and they got this guy sayin we got to pray and ask Jesus to forgive us our sins. Repent. So I think about it and figure the only thing I ever done that I really regret be the thing that put me in there the first place, so I ask Jesus to forgive me for that. And then I don't feel too bad, but I don't feel none better either. But what's the hurt, I figure? Maybe there's some truth in it. So I'm hedgin my bets. Figure if I go and get up there to Saint Peter at least I got that forgiveness going for me, right?

Martin stares at the man's feet, his red sneakers. Inhales some smoke, holds it, exhales into the wind.

I feel pretty good you know, the man continues. I aint never had no kids, just my screw-up brother's kids and his wife who I'd end up sendin money to whenever he landed himself in real trouble or took off. Funny, he such a bad guy and me, I work hard all my life and I'm the one gets sent up to the joint. Dint make no sense—but listen now. So the preacher guy tells me to pray for them, the kids, right? To pray for God to take care of them. So I says okay, figuring the same as before, but then I think, They good people, they go to church all the time so I don't much figure they need it. And I tell him I don't want to use up prayer time for someone I figure don't need it. So then he says I can pray for myself, pray for strength to do the things I want to do when I get outta there. But I aint need no strength. I aint a young man, I aint climbing ladders and playing with wires no more. So I made a decision: figure I'm doing the prayin so I can pray how I please. And you know what I did? Son, I prayed for money. Ha! (Here he stretches out his hands and looks at the sky). Lord, hehe, I said, send me some money. Show me the money, Lord! If anything gonna for sure help me out when I get on the outside, it's gonna be money.

He looks at Martin again, serious.

But I dint believe in the Good Lord, you see. See, I dint need to believe in Jesus to get out of that prison. But now, I got to believe in Jesus to get outta prison all together, in general see. I need Him to set my heart free, you know? My heart needed to get out! And you know what happened? I kept on goin to the preacher guy and talking to him cuz he seemed a nice enough fellow, and he had kids and would tell me how they were doin and all that and I like hearin that sort of thing. I'm an old man, I love birthdays and stuff. Then this one day, couple days before I'm set to get out I go to take out my money from the prisoner account and I was s'posed to have just forty-some dollars in there, and I come to find they's over three thousand! And I called the veteran's affairs office and social security and all anybody I could think of done put that money there. And that night instead of prayin for money I prayed and asked where that money come from. And you know what I realized? It was the good Lord. He told me, Jimmy, my man, here's three grand. You need it more than I do so you go out and you get yourself set free and enjoy the rest of your life. So I come out and give a thousand bucks to my brother's wife, give a thousand to my old work buddy who picked me up from the jail so I could stay with him for awhile—he has an extra room, see—and I give most of the other thousand to a church cuz I got other money comin' in from the veterans and from social security and so I figure I give back what I don't need.

So what do you think about that then? the old man asks.

Martin's head hurts. His eyes hurt. He misses his grandfather, misses whatever it was he had when his grandfather was alive that made it so he would never feel jealous of a man like this. But here he is, shaking with jealousy, jealousy and a great desire to be filled up with love, either by some thing or for some thing. The Good Lord be damned, he will take *any*thing! An image in his head: the gold-plated bowl of holy water at the funeral. He had dipped his fingers in, tentatively, crossed himself. It had been years since he'd been to church, and he took Communion at the funeral service, realizing the mistake of that only after. Is ignorance an excuse for offending God? If you take Communion but forgot you should go to confession first, does that count? God shouldn't be that strict, but where would ignorance end as an excuse? Is not knowing the difference between Good and Evil a get-out-of-Hell-free card ?

> OLD MAN: I said what do you think about that?
> PLAYWRIGHT: *Surprised, pulled from an imagining.* What?
> OLD MAN: I said so what do you think about that? God paid me three grand just to believe inem!
> PLAYWRIGHT: *Looks around. No joggers. A different skateboarder. PLAYWRIGHT stands in front of OLD MAN for a beat, hands in pockets. Then mutters.* Well, have a good day,
> *Exit playwright down the street to the bank.*

He has just over three thousand dollars in his checking account. Could he buy a tabernacle with that? Could he buy a gym membership and jogging gear?

He should forgive Claire. She's asked him to, to take her back. He should.

He takes out a hundred dollars, and walks around the block, looking back at the old man, still sitting on the brick wall, still trying to get people to stop. Come and listen to the Good Lord! the man shouts to the traffic, laughing, letting his meaty legs and red sneakers swing.

Martin finds a window seat in the diner on Second Avenue. Thinking about his grandfather, his grandmother, Claire—he lifts the corner of the huge laminated menu, lets it fall back. He rubs his palm across his face, small beads of sweat on his upper lip. Stirs his spoon in the glass of ice water, wipes the drips off the menu with a napkin. This whole section of the diner is lined with windows that open in the summertime to let in the warm breezes and street noise. Not warm enough just yet: the windows are closed.

There was an article he read in the *Herald Tribune* over a year ago, on a trip to Paris he and Claire took together. A bomb had gone off in a market in Baghdad and killed three people. He remembers Claire showing it to him, sitting outside a tourist newsstand near Notre Dame. Three killed, but over a hundred injured. They never go into the details of injuries, he'd thought. Later they found an internet café and he looked up the details. Learned about something called organic shrapnel-- pieces of an exploded suicide-bomber that bury themselves in the skin of survivors. Weeks later, the survivors find bumps in their skin. Like finding your undeveloped twin's fetus in your neck—he saw that in a movie once.

Martin sees a fruit stand from the window, a tiny market, young couples pushing strollers. Any one of those babies could be a bomb in disguise, he thinks. A fake baby stuffed with explosives. Or a real baby that explodes, the tiny teeth digging into his neck as fast as bullets. He remembers an image from a book about the childhood of Ayman al-Zawahri, thousands of teenage boys throwing themselves into gunfire on an Afghan battlefield, the bodies piling into a mountain reaching up toward paradise, how one boy knelt down over a fallen brother and wept with joy or jealousy for his friend who had died, been blessed with Heaven and its promise of virgins. The point was to die and ascend to paradise. At the time, Martin had thought it seemed so idiotic, so sublimely stupid. But now he thinks: at least they had a purpose. Their lives were short, but they were definitive. He orders a spinach omelet with feta and spoons ice into the hot coffee the Greek waitress brings. At the table in front of him an old man and a five-year-old girl start getting up to leave. Martin eyes them; must be a granddaughter.

Excuse me, Martin asks, Any chance I can have the hot sauce?

The old man turns. Sure thing, he says, smiles, and standing he hands the red bottle to Martin. Pulling on his jacket he asks, You want the paper too? He produces a folded *Post* from the jacket's breast pocket.

Yeah, that'd be great, thanks. You sure?

Of course, no problem. We're heading to a movie, aren't we honey?

The girl nods and smiles. Martin looks at her and smiles back.

Well, you have a nice afternoon, Martin says.

You too son, the man says, and they're gone.

Martin shakes the hot sauce and unfolds the paper. Picture of the Iranian president, Yankees' and Mets' scores, public school initiative. The same old. He starts eating and picks up the saint book again with the other hand. A sentence from the life of Saint Denis comes back to him. *Over the centuries, believers have seen the image of the Saint walk down the Montmartre hill, have watched him walk down the Mount of Martyrs, all the way to the Seine.* People killing for their religion, people dying for their religion, people getting paid to believe in a religion—Martin has the urge to cry. His grandfather is gone. Gone to a God Martin doesn't believe in, or simply gone.

If only bits of that body had lodged themselves deep into Martin, so that he'd have that love, always, growing in him.

There was a time, years ago, when Martin walked in on his sick grandfather, kneeling, praying an Our Father. Martin stood in the doorway and listened. His grandfather's Parkinson jaw shook, and Martin heard him muttering the words *kingdom* and *glory*, heard him asking for the good Lord to protect Martin, his dead son's son, who, Dear Lord, will need His protection more than anyone.

1

I went off the deep end. Went way into it. Not that what happened was Margot's fault, or that it was David Elliott's, either. But I had been a critic. A critic looking at beauty always with a dose of cynicism like you have to if you're going to be any good. Harold Bloom says that all a critic can give, as a critic, is deadly encouragement to artists (poets, he was talking about), and always remind them how important art is, how great the responsibility of the artist. One of the differences between Margot and I was that she didn't consider what I did to be art. Poetry, lyrics, fiction: that can be art, she said. But writing about art? There's just no way you can make a piece of writing more successful than the original object you're writing about, the truer object. But I think it's like Nietzsche said: there are no facts, just interpretations. Subjectivity rules all, etcetera—and by facts I think he means real things, objects, exactly what Margot was arguing is the "truer" art. My PD, my psych doc, he tells me I was attracted to her because she knew what she wanted—to be an artist, however she defined it—whereas I thought I was already being one, it just depended on another level of interpretation. And that's exactly it, the PD says; I had to look at what I did a certain way in order to feel okay about it. And I knew this. I knew I had to convince myself. Not just about her but about everything. If I had something I wanted to say about music or art, drugs made it easier to find the right words. The world, my PD told me, is all about perception, how you look at things. No shit, Spivey, I said. And that was that. Since then I've been reading some Sartre I found in the library here, and you now how he said Hell is other people? I'm sitting in this fucking hospital and I swear to you it's worse than *No Exit*. Some kind of cruel joke, keeping that book in a mental hospital library. Anyway. Art, if you think about it in terms of Nietzsche and Sartre and Hell and God and Nature, art is just something changing interpretation. The object itself isn't art, it's the interpretation. I mean, Sontag defined art as stylized, dehumanized representation, and I think she's right. It's the neurons firing, the electricity of the mind changing direction. The position, not the disposition, she would say. That's the art. I thought about this and asked my PD if he thought about prescribing drugs as an art. He said: Hmmmmmmm, I'm not sure. And I said, Because, you know, that makes everything I see a work of art. And then he just looked at me like Margot used to, and said I needed to calm down.

2

Margot was a student at UW, the University of Washington. I met her at the Crocodile three years ago, in Seattle, at a show we were both writing about—me for the Weekly, and her for the U's paper. I'd already noticed her at shows around town, taking pictures with a crappy pocket digital. She had blonde hair with this black streak where she'd dyed a portion about an inch wide, so she was easy to notice. It was a Negative-Sontag, that's what I called it. The opposite of Susan Sontag's hair, that black with a white stripe. So I went over to her once. I'm Eddie, I said, holding out a hand. Margot, she said. Your hair, I told her, it's a Negative-Sontag. And she was quiet and looked me up and down. Then she said, Listen, Eddie. I don't mean to be rude, but I'll buy you a beer if you don't talk to me any more tonight, deal? And she didn't say anything else so I agreed. Deal, I said. She bought me a Rainier and I wandered away. Like Bloom says, Sometimes one succeeds, sometimes one fails. I kept watching for her during the band's set, but the band was sucking so I did a few lines in the bathroom and got in a fight with someone's drummer, threw him into one of the stalls. Something he said, and then he had his face against the urinal and I had cut my hand on half a bottle, the bottom half. I remember I could lift my palm up like a piece of cloth, had to get a bunch of stitches. I never did take well to coke.

3

Freud says something like this: A belligerent state permits itself any misdeed that will disgrace the individual. But Margot and I kept running into each other at shows, and I remember the next time I saw her I said, I guess I owe you a beer, Negative-Sontag, and she asked what had happened to my hand, since it was all bandaged. I made something up, I didn't want to scare her or make her think I was some dangerous drug addict fuck-up. I read this thing she wrote in the UW paper about a visiting photography professor and thought she was an okay writer, but I wanted to impress her—Anatomy is destiny, Freud said—so I gave her the number of the arts editor at the Stranger, so she could see about doing a feature on the professor for them. It was a good gig for a college student, a good clip for the portfolio; I guess that's why she wanted to be my friend at first. Some nights she'd come by my apartment and we'd smoke up together and fool around, it was always her idea. I would get so high sometimes that it would feel like it was all a dream, like she'd never even come over at all. I'd usually pass out, and when I'd wake up she'd be gone. Once I woke up and looked at my stash and we'd gone through more weed than I thought two people could possibly smoke together. Still though, my PD asks me if I think she might have been stealing from me, but I don't think she would have. I black out sometimes, I explain. And, yeah, you know what Nietzsche would say: Ah, women. They make the highs higher and the lows more frequent.

4

If we believe Sontag when she said that to photograph is to confer importance, then Margot's professor, David Elliott, was one hell of a photographer. I'd read about him in the arts sections of newspapers, and he was part of this review in The New Yorker once. He had a Guggenheim fellowship, academia fame. And he looked just like that in the photos of him: a young and somewhat famous person who could afford to drink good expensive Scotch and maintain his status as 'artist.' Everything about him conferred importance. The show Margot wanted to write about was at one of those hipster galleries in Belltown. A place that made good money sentimentalizing the neighborhood's past, whatever had existed before the gentrification that birthed the gallery in the first place—illness strikes men when they are exposed to change, Herodotus said—and these places, they'll put a graffitied bathroom stall behind UV-protected glass, or arrange one of Kurt Cobain's smashed guitars behind a velvet rope to try and make it look all haphazard and natural. I saw the *Stranger* arts editor having drinks one night at a place near the gallery and went in to talk to him. Margot had sent him some clips. Margot's a good writer, I told him. She can do it. A little obsessed with Didion, but I guess it's a phase we all go through. I laughed. Sounds great, the editor said. An Elliott piece would be good. Margot says she's related to him or has a class with him or something? Yeah, I said. Great, the editor said. Elliott's stuff's great. Then the editor got up and left to meet someone. Great. Everything was fucking great to these editors.

5

Yes, I'm in a hospital now. Call no man happy until he's dead, Herodotus said. I'm at Western State, in Tacoma, where Frances Farmer, the Hollywood actress from the '40's, where she once stayed for electro-shock treatments. They've written books about her. Kurt Cobain even wrote a song about her, called "Frances Farmer Will Have Her Revenge On Seattle." It's on Nirvana's *In Utero* record. A beautiful record. I miss the comfort of being sad, he sings. I should really write something about that while I'm here, I think. Or not. Maybe if I can get my thoughts straight I will. That would be a good thing for me to do. Raymond Carver said he never wrote a line worth a nickel when he was drunk, so maybe it'll be good for me to try writing clean. But if you ask me, that sounds like something you only admit when you're completely wasted.

6

I was a good critic. They didn't give me enough credit. In the month after the feature was published, when Margot and Elliott were working on her video project, she dyed her hair all black (no more Negative-Sontag), started drinking coffee instead of beer when I saw her at shows, and was harder to find around town. What's more, her musical tastes shifted back a decade. When I did see her, when she came by and did blow and fucked me, I always wanted to ask why she never stayed in the morning. She was embarrassed by me, which is fine, I guess. But every time I ran into her she kept pretending she didn't know me like she did, like she hadn't ever been to my place. Then there was the hair change, and the coffee, and I knew she was cheating on me with him, with David Elliott. I confronted her about her fucking infidelities in the alley outside a show. You whore, I said. You know what Kant would have told you? A lie annihilates the dignity of man. That's what he would have said.

7

I went to the gallery in Belltown for opening night of her group show. I had gotten kind of fucked up on coke beforehand because I was so nervous about seeing her. I hadn't seen her in a few weeks at least, and I missed her. She had stopped coming over, and so I'd just get high by myself and listen to Bauhaus until I fell asleep. She hadn't even told me she was in a group show, I had to read about it in the listings. I went to see her and her collaboration with Elliott, this video piece, her art, that was nine 13-inch television screens stacked three-by-three against the back wall of the gallery, with some videos playing, I can't remember. When I first saw her she was talking to the gallery owner, all smiles and gesticulation. Then, when Margot saw me, she smiled, kind of nervous, but still a smile. I started walking over and she looked over my shoulder and pointed at me and then suddenly there was this big security bear of a guy telling me to get the hell out. I looked back for her but she was gone, so I stood there looking at the security guy—we were in an art gallery, he wasn't going to get too physical surrounded by art—and I finished my beer slowly, then pocketed a full one, him following close with a paw on my shoulder as I walked out. When I was outside I turned and watched through the big glass windows. The security guard stood at the door, lit a cigarette, watched me. I spotted black-haired Margot through the glass again, still talking to the gallery owner. Then I saw David Elliott for the first time, the first time in person, emerge from the storage room or some other place. He was wearing a CBGB t-shirt under a velvet blazer. He walked over to Margot and she pointed at me behind the glass. He smiled and waved like a priest.

8

I wandered down to First Avenue. All truly great thoughts are conceived by walking, I said to myself. Nietzsche had said that, and also that for a woman and man to form a friendship, there must exist a little antipathy, and I hoped this was just a phase. I passed the editor who'd published the original feature Margot'd written—it had been a damned good piece, Margot had become a good writer, I'll give her that—and I waved hello, then held my fingers to my lips to say I was going out for cigarettes. He gave me a thumbs-up. I kept walking. Great thoughts, great thoughts, I mantraed. I walked a long ways, all the way downtown to the market, sipping from the beer I kept in my jacket pocket. I passed the Showbox, where I was supposed to review this new Portland band the following night, and then headed for the strip club just down the block, stopping in a self-pay parking lot to trash the bottle and smoke half a joint I'd found in the pocket with the beer. The proper task of life is art! I screamed to no one in particular. Then, in the club I ordered the most expensive Scotch—your most expensive Scotch! I demanded—and sat down next to the stage. The dancer was a skinny girl who looked like my best friend in grade school. Massive Attack was playing loud over the house speakers, all bass and heavy thumps, the song that goes, You are my angel, come from way above to give me love. I could see the skinny dancer's sternum between tubular breasts hanging like socks full of pennies. She wiggled toward me with a dumb expression that betrayed nothing more than that she'd been doing this for a long time, and that she knew how to separate who she was here from who she was outside. I drank the whole Scotch at once, and thought how Bukowski had said that sometimes you just have to kick the whole bloated sensation of art out on its whore-ass. I wanted to scream again, and as I took a deep breath, I felt a burn and tightening in my chest. Then a sharp pain, piercing in time with the thumping of the bass in the song, and an image of Margot and David Elliott pressed together in the gallery storage room, black flames licking the walls. David Elliott was taking pictures of her, hanging them developing from a rope that ended in a noose, and that noose was being pulled over my own dick. What would Freud have said? What would Sontag? My heart was like a fist punching from the inside. I stared at the dancer and thought of peeling her skin away, what might be in there. Pennies in her breasts. I watched her coming toward me—dumb, blank, I loved her, I hated her, I loved her—and I was sweating and shaking, could feel my face turning color. I wanted it to stop. Margot was screaming in my head, getting fucked to the beat of the music. The dancer swayed. She was doing this to me. The noose tightened. I don't know how, but the dancer, or the bartender, they'd poisoned the Scotch or something, David Elliott had paid them. I slammed the glass down under my hand, felt it break. I stood and the dancer was looking at me, not with the dumb look now, but like I'd peeled off the face and here was this little girl. A little girl to love. Sontag says pornography isn't about sex but is about death. Was I about to die? I remember the girl trying to cover herself as I stepped on the stage, and I remember the music was playing, loud and thick and beautiful, when they carried me out, covered in blood, singing like a king on their shoulders, and I remember now, sitting here and thinking back on everything, what Freud would have said: one is very crazy when in love.

fig. 1

fig. 2

fig. 3

November 23, 2009

Something about Happiness

The HAPPINESS *play is short: three acts, no intermission. It begins on a Tuesday, election day, moves to a rooftop party that evening, and ends the following morning around a breakfast table. Act One ends with the 'car accident,' and Act Two begins with Patrick and Claire getting back to the apartment (the giant noise and light's going out at the end of Act One isn't explained, and I guess we're just taken to assume it was something of a psychological moment for both of them—whatever it is, I think the sound will work at scaring and confusing the audience into a state perhaps closer to that the characters are meant to be inhabiting). Back at the apartment Patrick and Claire go to an election night party on the roof of the apartment building. The sister's friends are there, mostly artist-types and young professionals. Patrick doesn't have friends there; I guess it's assumed he's still too new in town to know anyone beyond his sister. One of her friends there is a glass blowing artists who makes his living selling glass sculptures at the Pike Place Market and giving classes at a studio in Fremont. He also shows his own artwork occasionally (it doesn't sound any better than Margot's stuff, but it sounds like something a person in Seattle would do, and it works well enough in the play). The artist fairly blatantly is hitting on Claire, telling her about his new art project called "Laos, Christmas 2007," which involves 251 glass neon blue Christmas trees, one for each of the children that died, on average, of starvation in Laos that year. He tells Claire and Patrick that the work is going to be on exhibition that December. Patrick asks if the artist has ever been to Laos, and when he says, No, but he has plans to go, there's a wonderful 'beat' in the text that Simon obviously left there for audience laughter. This is a part of the play I think I like more than I should just out of personal bias (fucking David Elliott). I'm fairly certain this Martin Patrick Simon guy and I would get along well.*

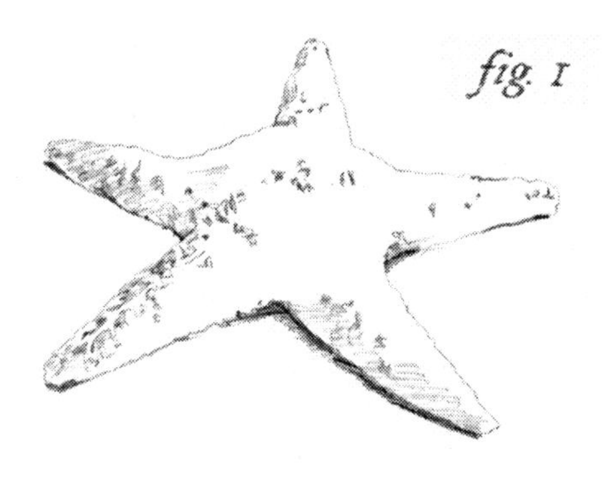
fig. 1

It was because we spoke of Leonard Cohen together—that was why I brought the boy home with me. I was playing *Songs of Love and Hate* on the house speakers behind the bar at Flanagan's and whenever I went to ask if he'd like another whiskey he made a comment about Leonard Cohen. Young. Twenty-three, maybe twenty-four. I am not much older but he seems young when I think of myself at that age, when I think of what happened to me when I was twenty-two and what brought me here to Asheville. Wisdom suddenly at twenty-two, wiser now at twenty-nine. Not quite thirty, and that makes me think of the Thirty Years War, makes me think of the age of Christ when he started preaching. Still uncomfortable thinking of myself as an adult, as a grown woman. But wise, yes, experienced. I can hear him snoring in the other room. *New Skin...* was his favorite record, he said. He liked the Chelsea Hotel song. Getting head on an unmade bed, he quoted. It's a nice rhyme, I said, and smiled. Snores. I can't sleep. Not because of the snores—I can hear him over the rain, though—but I had to leave the bed, come here to cry. What is it about my own bathroom? Personal, safe, like a hiding place when you're a kid. The only room more personal and safe than your own bedroom is your own bathroom, I think. Never mind what might have happened. Sitting on your own toilet, staring out your own window, listening to the rain through the snores. It's your own grain-of-sand perspective on the world. I'm sitting here like a character in a song, wanting to cry, but not being able to. She snuck out of bed, slept on the toilet instead. Cohen could sing it just like that. A sad girl wanting just to want something, looking out the window, body numb like a coming heart attack. She chokes like she's going to cry but can't. Strange. Draft in my face from the window is nice, humid smells. The sky is gray over the parking lot, the moon covered in scar-like rain clouds. Summer smells. Crickets buzzing faint in the rain. Or rain buzzing faint on the crickets. Distant black Carolina hills, the streetlamp in the parking lot like a sun in their universe, the buzzing mosquitoes around it like moons. Thoughts at quarter to three in the morning. I don't know why this, why that, why it isn't or wasn't easier, why I can't enjoy it. I want to. I miss the joy, the sense of love, the pressure of a man lying on top of me. Embracing, moving, warm affection, grace. It's not fear anymore, I don't think. There was a time I was afraid just to go into bars. Paralysis. A man touching me would have been hell. What happened to me had happened in a bar, in someone else's bathroom, and so now I work in a bar. It is a way of confronting that recurring nightmare, I think. I remember I thought he was helping me. I had stumbled to the bathroom to throw up, we were both so drunk, and he followed me and I thought he was coming to hold back my hair, and I saw everything that was about to happen, and then I watched him as he did it to me. Now I think maybe I can replace him with the faces of better lovers, but when I think thoughts like that I find myself seeming naïve, and I feel like I'm an embarrassment to women, that I should be strong and driven and get over it. I read an article by Mariane Pearl, the woman whose reporter husband was captured and decapitated in Iraq. She is a strong woman. The film of her husband's decapitation was on YouTube. Pearl said she would never watch it but I wonder still if she did. I picture her as a strong, Balzacian writer after seeing her husband killed, watching herself be widowed on the internet. I admire her. I read an article she wrote about how one in three women on an Indian reservation report being sexually assaulted. Report. Twice as many in reality, you have to figure. Two in three. For the rest of America the number is one in six. I knew that statistic. So it's twice as worse for the reservations. Federal-regulated hells. She wrote about an agency on a Sioux reservation that was established to help these women. What I remember most about the article was how one girl had had it happen to her in her early teens, and then in her late teens she confronted her attacker. Just went up to him and spoke. What did she say? The article wasn't specific, and I cannot imagine. What do you say to someone who did that to you? What would you say to the person who chopped off your husband's head? I don't know. These are strong women. I have read strong words from women, words that could blow the walls off buildings, but I have never encountered a woman as strong as the girl in the article. One in six, one in three. More than that really, you have to figure. Are we all like this, I wonder? Are we all paralyzed to it? I am not afraid anymore. I AM NOT. I took this job at the bar because I don't know where my attacker is, I cannot walk up to him and say things. It is my presence, my presence in the world without being afraid, THAT is my confrontation, THAT is bigger than any words to him. But still. It has been years now. Years and I cannot enjoy it. The boy snoring on the other side of the door, naked, sweaty, still wearing his socks. We talked about Leonard Cohen, we kissed, I invited him back. I liked talking to him. I like him still. I like his skinny arms and the way he bites his lower lip when he gets nervous. But can he like me back? He is snoring out there in my bed, finished, and I am in here in my bathroom, thinking. I am becoming sad. But I think that all I can do is keep trying. Keep living. There's a poem by Leonard Cohen where he writes that his diary is more glorious than the Bible, so I am looking for what he must have found in his diary as I write this. I am looking for God in these words. I search this world and am finding only myself and that terrifies me. I do not think it is because of what happened to me, but because I am not as strong as the teenage girl in that article. I have to do something. I have to do something to get stronger, strong as a woman who could chop off the head of a villain. I have to believe in God again. Or denounce God again. Where are you my God? If you are the love that you claim to be, then come down through the clouds and shatter that yellow streetlamp. Stand in the rainy driveway as an angel, as an apparition, as a supernatural. Because I am dying here like this. I am dying, and I am young.

Unhappy families find unhappiness in their own ways. It's that second line of *Anna Karenina* Martin's thinking about when he enters the grocery on east 108th street in Manhattan. His wife, two blocks away at Mt. Sinai Hospital, is sitting, staring, dumb with grief at the sight of Anna, their first daughter, spending her 16th day on this planet under observation in some sort of incubator in the neo-natal unit. A plastic box with a light and tubes, something like what his cousins once kept their pet gerbils in when he was growing up. Anna, this little non-gerbil, the missing piece to make Martin and Claire a family, finally, after everything that had happened. Now that piece was lying unmoving in a plastic box like a transparent coffin. They named her Anna after Martin's mother, long since passed away in a car accident that also took his father. His grandparents having passed in recent years as well, it was only the cousins he had to call with the news. It's Martin, in New York, your cousin. Yes, a little girl. Yes, early. I think so. The doctors are doing what they can, but they say it will be okay. Yes, yes. Yes, they said she'll be fine. We'll bring her out soon as we can. Anna Catherine. Yes, after my mom. Thanks, you too. Say hi to your kids for me. Bye.

It wasn't okay, of course. Unhappy families may not be alike, but unhappiness, after awhile, can be. Anna was born six weeks early, and the umbilical cord had wrapped around her neck like some bloody noose. She was blue when she came out. He wasn't supposed to see that, and he told Claire he didn't. But she was blue. This cold, blue alien thing weighing barely four pounds. If only there were some other family's unhappiness he can trade for.

It's cold in Manhattan. Strangely cold for October. The wind biting, everyone in their coats and gloves. In just a dirty shirt and jeans Martin's come outside for air, headed for the grocery store the nurse smoking by the doors told him was just down the block. Claire finally fell asleep in one of the orange chairs the nurses set up next to Anna. When she woke she found Martin leaned back, staring into the incubator as if it were nothing at all, listening to music on his headphones. She tapped him on the knee and made him leave. *Go get us some real food,* she whispered through the beeps and hisses of the small respirator attached to their daughter's face. *See if you can smuggle in some Indian. Baluchi's or something.*

I'm not hungry, he said.

Me neither. But we have to eat. We can go down to the cafeteria. Get out of this room. The nurses will keep an eye on her.

No. I don't want us to leave her.

I know, sweetie. She leaned over and ran a hand through his greasy hair. He tried to smile, staring at the deep purple circles under her bloodshot eyes.

Hon, I—he started to say.

She put her hand on his cheek. Just go and get us some food, she said. We'll eat and then we'll come back and she'll still be here.

Martin nodded. He got up, kissed Claire on the forehead, walked out the door without looking at the baby. A tumor in his chest all the way to the elevator. *We'll come back and she'll still be here.* Once in the elevator he focused on the people around him, the people who, maybe, had it worse in this hospital than he did.

Get up, get food, abandon daughter in the plastic box, come back, get wife, eat food, go back to room with the gerbil tubes, keep sitting with daughter, and wait. But what are they waiting for? She would be okay or she wouldn't be okay. That's what it was: they were waiting for a doctor to come in and say, *She's okay; you can rip out the tubes and go home now.*

But even then.

Martin shakes his head and shoves his hands in his pockets as he trudges down Madison Avenue. She's just so fucking *tiny.*

Martin walks to the counter. He'd asked the nurse by the doors where he could get a pack of cigarettes and here he is, buying a pack. It's been 6 months since he last smoked. An hour after Claire told him they were pregnant he went out on the street, lit a final Dunhill, and gave the rest of the pack to a homeless man going through the sidewalk trash for aluminum cans. That was a happy moment. Claire and he were going to have a child, a little boy or girl. They were going to be a family. A happy family, the three of them. It had seemed the opposite of watching your whole life flash before your eyes—he saw an entire future project before him, a life of private school interviews, of orchestra and band recitals, of sports and birthday parties, of eating out on Friday nights at whatever favorite restaurant they would share as a family. Family vacations, family portraits, family trees. His heart had pounded with excitement, and he'd thrown the half-smoked butt at the street and ran back up the stairs to grab his wife. Now he reaches for the yellow pack of cigarettes pushed towards him across the counter and heads back into the cold.

Martin and Claire were married in Seattle, at Gas Works Park, skyline and mountains in the distance. They took a few days between the wedding and leaving for Maui on their honeymoon, staying in the Four Seasons downtown and spending lazy mornings with room service in the linen sheets, leaving the hotel only for drinks and dinner at the Pink Door. One of these days they took Dorothy, the seven-year-old daughter of Martin's cousin Josh, to the Seattle Aquarium. They were all—Martin and Claire, Josh, his wife Ellen, Dorothy—going out to dinner that evening, but Josh had some work to finish in the office and Ellen wanted to get some shopping done for Dorothy's coming birthday. So Martin and Claire offered to watch her for an afternoon.

It went unsaid that Martin and Claire thought of the afternoon as a hypothetical. Trial run. Dorothy was the perfect little girl of young adult novels, a pigtailed bookworm, all curiosity and politeness. The three of them held starfish together, made *Ewww-ing* noises at the octopus, tapped the glass at the shark tank. Dorothy and Claire got along particularly well, and there's a picture Martin took of the two of them on a shelf in their apartment, Claire holding up Dorothy to look at the seahorses, their faces blue with the glow of the tank. *I used to love seahorses when I was your age,* he remembers Claire telling Dorothy. *I wanted to be like Ariel in the Little Mermaid, and have a seahorse to ride all over the ocean. I'd name him Charlie.* Martin remembers Dorothy laughed and said, *You should name the seahorse after Uncle Martin. Because his face is like a horse.* They all laughed.

Martin smokes his way through the pack on a bench across the street from the hospital. He knows he's supposed to go get food, but he's still not hungry. He knows Claire doesn't want to eat either. She only wanted some time alone with the baby, some time alone to talk to the doctors, to see if they'll tell her something different when she's alone than they would tell the couple when they were together. He knows this is what she's doing because he's done the exact same thing since the first day of the waiting.

The first day Anna was in the box with the tubes he kept thinking about that moment with Dorothy and the seahorse. The doctor had pulled Martin aside while Claire was sleeping. She still didn't know the baby wasn't perfect.

I don't want to lie to you, the doctor said. *Your daughter's brain was without oxygen. Now—there's a chance that there will be brain damage. I don't want to scare you, we don't know much yet. We've put her under observation in the neonatal unit. It's one of the best in the country. We're just going to have to wait and see.* The doctor looked Martin in the eye when he told him this. Martin appreciated that.

What do you mean by 'brain damage'? Martin asked. *Is she going to live?*

Like I said, the doctor repeated, we're going to have to just wait and see. She was born early, and one never knows what's going to happen while the brain's still developing. There's a chance she could be completely normal.

But there's a bigger chance she won't be normal?

Well—

Are you telling me she's going to be retarded?

There's a chance there could be some impairment, yes.

But we have to wait and see.

Yes.

How long?

I'd say we should know more within a few days.

16 days later and they don't know anything more. The doctor has stopped looking at him in the eyes when he says, *We just have to keep waiting.*

The seahorse always seemed like a strange animal to Martin. He was never really sure where they were found in real life. It seems like something so strange would have to exist only in the deep, deep Pacific. Or somewhere in the tropics, where all the fish are odd colors and odd shapes, where strangeness is expected and perfectly normal. Anna, if she ever gets out of that plastic box, is going to come out like a seahorse. He's certain of this.

He's been listening to music a lot at the hospital. After a week passed and there was no change—she had gained a little weight, but not as much as they would have liked—he went home to pick up some clean clothes for Claire and him. He brought back his iPod. The patterns of beeps and hisses had become too much to listen to. It was like some machine was making his daughter, different from all the other children being born upstairs. The children that got to go home. Anna shared her birthday with at least one other little girl—in the room next to theirs. Martin had met that father in the hall, shared congratulations with him. That little girl had already met the rest of her family, was going on the third week of a happy life somewhere, part of one of all those same happy families in the world. And Anna was still here, still being made, still a stranger to the world, still not quite part of it. Had she even been born yet, really? If she died now, would that still be considered a stillbirth? She can't breathe on her own. She was born without oxygen in her brain. Isn't that death? Isn't whatever *life* these machines breathe into her manufactured. Those beeps and hisses.

It's too much to think about, too much to listen to, and so Martin listens to music when he sits with his daughter. The music of his happy adolescence and teenage years, in the hopes that if Anna is surrounded by more happiness, well, that might help some tiny bit. He sits listening to Elliott Smith, Calvin Johnson, Pearl Jam. And the music his parents listened to, too, he thinks, based on the cassettes they left. Van Morrison, Steely Dan, Pink Floyd. The Stones, Beatles. Sitting on the bench, lighting another cigarette, he slips the headphones into his ears. *Exile On Main Street* was in the car when they died.

A song by Nirvana comes up on the shuffle. From their *In Utero* record: "Frances Farmer Will Have Her Revenge On Seattle." That actress, a perfect character for a Cobain-penned song. Born in Seattle, she'd been declared legally insane and taken a nose-dive from Hollywood fame to the Western State mental hospital, an institution Martin's grandfather had actually helped build when he worked as a carpenter. Martin directed a production of a play about her in college. In a famous fictional biography, Western State was the setting for her lobotomy and rape. No one really knows the truth, if she was or wasn't. In the play she was.

There was a point when he and Claire were dating, when she missed a period and there was talk of abortion. He never fully considered it, but at that stage, only twenty-two years old, neither of them could truly conceptualize the idea of a child. And now with Anna, it's different but he feels the same.

Even only slight retardation, that's basically the same as insane, isn't it? Isn't it just the brain not working right, like Frances Farmer? So best case, if she lives, Anna may be another Frances Farmer. Subject of a rock song, Hollywood starlet, eventual laundry woman and lobotomized mental hospital sex slave.

When Martin directed the play about Ms. Farmer in college he was excited to use the rape version of her life. He thought it was more interesting, the greater unhappiness to contrast with the grand happiness of stardom.

What would his father think of him?

His grandfather? His mother and grandmother?

What would Claire think of him?

And Anna? Will Anna ever be able to think of him? Will she meet God, and the two of them look down from Heaven and judge him?

Martin waits to cross the avenue and sees a pizza place on the corner. Maybe the smell will be enough to take their minds off everything for a few minutes. His hands hurt when he reaches in his pockets, almost burning. Cold cracked skin against his jeans.

Back inside he has to ask a nurse to go and get Claire. He's not allowed to bring the pizza into the room with the boxes and tubes.

I'll go get her, Mr. Simon, the nurse says, all empathy, and walks quietly down the beeping, sterile hallway.

Claire comes walking back with a slight limp; she's been sleeping in a chair. She looks horrible, sweat stains on her gray t-shirt and the same dark, bloodshot eyes from earlier. She's all he has of this desperate, unhappy family.

I'm not hungry, she says. A weak smile.

Me neither. I thought we could, I don't know. Smell them at least. Martin puts his arm around her and they walk toward the elevator to go down to the cafeteria.

How is she?

I don't know, Claire answers.

She leans her head against his shoulder while they wait for the doors to open. You're cold, she says.

Yeah. It's freezing out. Did you talk to the doctor?

And you smell like smoke.

Did you—

He came by.

And?

He said *wait and see*.

Right. Martin nods and grips his wife's shoulder. It's going to be okay, he says flatly.

She's going to die, isn't she, Martin.

He wishes he could comfort her. Could grab her and look her square in the face and give her faith. Give her some hope that their daughter is going to be fine. He feels tears run.

I don't—I don't know, he says, choking, trying not to be the guy standing there crying when the elevator arrives. A guy holding a pizza box and crying.

The elevator makes a dinging sound. The doors open, close.

fig. 3

When I first get to the hospital they bring me in to see the doc and she asks me to tell her what I'm doing in her office. This is just where they brought me, I say. I know, she answers, but why did they bring you *here*, to this place? We both sit there quietly for a moment. She glances at the file in her hand and then stares at me. I look at her eyes and notice they're different colors—one blue, one green, and I think about my mother. She keeps staring and I think she is going to read my mind. But then she just looks down and reads to me from my file and waves to the orderlies. They have hands like stone that grip me hard, and they carry me to a different, colder room.

The next time they bring me to see the doc I am shaking and cold and try not to look at her eyes and I just start talking: There was this time, right before college, I tell her, hugging myself. It was the summer before. I went to the University of Washington, it should tell you that in the file. I pause, rub my hands together, and the doc nods. It's okay, she says, trying to make me comfortable, but she doesn't offer me the blanket on the back of her chair or even look at the file on the desk, the closed file with my name on the tab. I keep talking: A buddy and I went down to Westport to go salmon fishing. Must have been middle or late July because I remember we were going for Kings and Silvers. We borrowed his older brother's car and got him to buy us a case of Rainier and a case of Oly and we headed for the coast. We were going to go out on his dad's boat early the next morning. We drove down drinking and got to the ocean around sunset. We kept toasting the whole way down, To the last fishing trip! That was it, you know, that was going to be the last time. One last hurrah before my buddy went off to the marines like his dad and older brother, the one whose car we'd taken. I drove, I remember. My buddy just drank. He drank maybe three for every one I drank, because the transmission was fucked and it would only go from third to fourth at a certain rpm you had to search for with the stick shift. I asked him if he was sure he didn't want to drive, because it was his brother's car and I thought he'd be better at working the gears. It was an old VW bug, you ever have one of those, doc? Ran like shit but it was fun. My buddy, he said he'd rather just ride along, and if I kept driving that'd be just fine. I remember the car had a windshield that was right up in your face. The bugs would splatter against it and I could lean forward on the wheel and reach out the window and wipe the bugs off pretty easy. We got to Westport and drove south along the coast, out onto the Shoalwater Bay Reservation. This was before the casino and all that so the res was pretty dead, just some drunk stereotype Indians walking along the road, some kids playing basketball on a netless rim in a driveway, little convenience stores falling apart here and there. So I said, or maybe my buddy said, Let's go out on the beach, let's go watch the sunset. We could see the ocean off to the right of the highway and we found a service access road and drove out onto the sand. We weren't supposed to but it was low tide and the ground was hard and dark and wet enough and we spun the tires in it, kicking up these great shit-colored rooster tails I could watch falling in the rearview mirror.

I stop talking and look at the doc. I don't feel very good, I say. The doc nods. It's okay, she says again, but she still hasn't taken any notes. Don't you want to take notes? I ask her. No, I'm just listening, she says. I look at the file and think how my buddy would be dead in a couple years and I say, He was going to get sent to Afghanistan, my buddy. If he hadn't gotten killed there he probably would have had to go over to Iraq now and maybe that would have killed him. The doc nods. I wait for her to write down what I said. I think she should write down something like that; it seems important to write something like that down. I'm not going to take notes, she says, and I think she smiles a little bit. This bitch is reading my mind, I start to think, but before I finish the thought she says sweetly: I'm just listening, Eddie.

I watch the doc to see what she'll do next, if maybe she'll say something so I don't have to keep talking. I try to remember what I was saying but now all I can do is think of my buddy dying. I think about his eyes. What his eyes would have looked like at the moment when he died. They say the pupil expands to completely cover the iris, like a puddle of oil, until all the color has become just a dead black hole. I start to cry a little bit, and I don't say anything. The beach, the doc reminds me. You were talking about the beach. I wait for a bit, try to picture my buddy's eyes without deep black holes in them. But then I say, We drove around. I remember I got drunk. My buddy was really drunk by the time we got there. We ran out of cigarettes watching the sun set over the ocean and we smoked some weed in a glass pipe we found in the brother's glove compartment. I remember the ocean was incredible, the sun sort of melting into its own rippling reflection. I can remember that perfectly. A lot of things, a lot of trips with that buddy. I don't remember them very well. But I remember all those oranges and blues mixing, turning to make purples and reds. I felt, I don't know, I felt like this was what life was about. That this was something special. Being with a buddy, doing things you're not supposed to do. Driving illegally on a beach, drinking and smoking up on a res we're not supposed to be on. There was no reason. Just to do it, you know? You just did it because it was there. My buddy was going to go into the Marines because that's what his dad had done. I was going to go to college because I didn't have anything better and that was what I was supposed to do. I remember we stopped the car and watched the sun set into the west and I asked him if he was scared about joining up. We didn't know the country'd be over there yet, 9/11 wouldn't be for a couple years. But still I asked him if he was scared of getting killed, and he said he hadn't really thought about it. He just knew that was what he was supposed to do. I didn't understand that. I didn't understand it at all. We sat there for a long time thinking and bullshitting until it got completely dark. Finally I said, I don't really understand that. I don't really understand how you can just know, not if you haven't really thought about the dying part. If I were going to join up that would be all I could think about. He sat there and tapped the ashes out of the glass pipe and took the plastic baggy out of the glove box and filled it again. He held the lighter to the pipe and puffed and I asked if he thought he was supposed to join because his dad and brother wanted him to, but when he put the pipe down he choked out a no. It was his mother, he said. His mother had died a few years before, when he was still just a kid. He said sometimes at night, when he gets scared about the dying part, at those times he can hear his mother's voice: This is who you are. It's like my mother's singing, he said, still choking on the smoke, like a thousand sweet mothers singing, This is who you are. Whenever I wonder about it, it's just, This is who you are. This is who you are. This is who you are.

I've stopped shaking. The doc is leaning back in her chair and watching me. Me, I tell her, my dad worked on the Boeing assembly floor in Everett and my mom stayed home. That was it. There was no legacy there. After my buddy said what he said we tried to drive off the beach but the wheels had sunk in the wet sand. The tide was coming in and started to get worried the waves would come all the way up to where we were stuck. My buddy was just about passed out and I couldn't get the car out no matter how much I went from forward to reverse. The whole transmission was fucked at that point, and I kept yelling at him to wake the fuck up so we could get moving. He mumbled we should just sleep there. He passed out completely then, and I got out of the car and I ran down to the water to try and find a piece of driftwood or something to wedge under the tires as a lever. I could hear the waves but I couldn't see them. I tripped on something hard and fell and cut my hands on a broken shell, falling into a pile of seaweed. I remember I sat there in the slime for a few minutes and laughed at the situation and watched the stars and listened to the ocean. I tried to think about things I could study in college. I sat there and rubbed my legs and could feel the seaweed slime and blood running down my shins like a cold itch. I started to hate my buddy, just out of jealousy, you know? I was so pissed that he knew what he needed to do—and I didn't have a fucking clue. It didn't seem fair. Then in the distance I heard a noise that wasn't the ocean, and I saw this light coming towards me. I got terrified that I had died or that there was a spaceship or some crazy shit, but as it got closer I could see it was just another car. I ran over to the VW and turned on the hazards so they'd see we were there and it was this Jeep Wrangler with three guys in it a little older than us. They had open cans of PBR, were driving around on the beach just like we'd been except they had a stereo and blasting a Soundgarden record. They said they thought we were res cops at first, hiding in the dark. I told them what was going on and between the four of us—my buddy kept sleeping in the passenger seat—we were able to just each take a corner and lift the Bug right out of the sand and carry it onto more solid ground. My hands stung like hell from the shell gashes and salt water, and I remember I went over to the headlights of the jeep to look at them up close. They were all cut up and bleeding, like stigmata, and I wanted to ask my buddy if he remembered our Wednesday nights at the Catholic school, the catechism classes, but he was still sleeping in the car. I was pretty out of it by then too, especially once I realized we'd be okay from the tide and I let myself feel everything. I stumbled over to my sleeping buddy and screamed in his sleeping face through the closed window: Why hast thou forsaken me! The guys from the Jeep got quiet for a second and then just started laughing and turned up their music. My buddy didn't even wake up, just laid there reclined in the seat all peaceful like a plaster dead Jesus in Mary's arms. The rest of us drank what little beer we had left and passed the glass pipe around and we all fell asleep high on the beach, away from the tide. They were all students at UW, and we talked about meeting up when I got up there. The next morning I woke up in the sand next to the car and the jeep with UW guys was gone. My buddy and I were so hungover we never did make it to go fishing, just drove home. My buddy didn't remember anything about the jeep or moving the car, and I didn't tell him. I just told him I cut my hands tripping on a piece of driftwood when I went to take a piss. He didn't even notice that he'd been carried to a different place on the beach while he slept. Back on the road we bought some cheap cigarettes before leaving the res and just smoked and listened to whatever cassettes his brother had in the car the whole drive back. I remember I slipped a Screaming Trees tape into my pocket when my buddy wasn't looking, even though I didn't have a cassette deck anymore.

The doc leans forward in her chair and puts her hands together just like a concerned doctor should. I asked you to tell me what brought you here, she says. I rub my arms and shrug. She sighs and leans back and makes a note on her notepad. Then she waves to the orderlies and they gather me up with their freezing hands and take me away to my icy room, where I spend the rest of the day under the hard blue blankets, listening to my headphones and thinking about what I should have done different.

fig. 1

fig. 2

fig. 3

November 24, 2009

Something about H*APPINESS*

A bit of a recap: of course at the end of Act One Patrick and his sister Claire don't die by crashing into the apartment building. You think it's a car accident but you're not sure, and it doesn't really even matter because Act Two starts right away and you realize it was just a scare, a near-accident that served to remind them of their parents accident and the starting-over they've had to do with their lives. Act Two, then, introduces the artist character and there's the party on the roof, and it ends finally with Patrick going back downstairs to his sister's apartment saying he's going to turn in. He leaves his sister in the foreboding company of the Christmas tree artists who seems to represent evil even in just the tone Simon uses for stage directions; that act ends with Claire and the artist making out and going downstairs together (to fuck, presumably). Act Three opens with the brother, Patrick, lying alone on his bed and delivering a monologue. In the stage directions describing Patrick on the bed, I like how the playwright is careful to stress that the actor is not delivering the monologue to the audience but rather 'to himself, to God, to whomever it is we talk to when we are alone.' Then comes

Patrick's story. He remembers getting the phone call that his parents had died while he was at college in New Jersey (Princeton, I assume, because of the way he talks about 'giving up on opportunities to move out here' during Act One). Patrick is an aspiring poet, we learn, and after hearing his parents have died, (it was Claire, of course, who called), after the initial shock he discovers that he feels a sense of GRATITUDE for their death. Naturally, this depresses him. Like most young writers, he's sought to emulate the greats he admired, taking up smoking and heavy drinking as a way of combating his natural depression; his parents' death contributes to this depressive biography that seems, to him, a necessity for becoming a great writer. (This makes sense, Spivey—if you really think about it). He goes for a walk, thinking about Wordsworth, I would think, and thinking about his parents and what he is going to do now. That's when he realized, Patrick tells us, (rising from the bed), while he was walking down some train tracks, that he doesn't want to be sad. *He wants to be a great writer, but he doesn't WANT to have to be SAD! He wants to be a great writer, but he doesn't want to have to BE SAD to be GREAT. It seems like a great revelation the way it's worded in Simon's text. And it depresses him—Patrick, I mean—because all those writers he has admired the most have had such terrible lives. He doesn't want to live a terrible life, but at the same time the only HAPPY life he can imagine for himself involves that self becoming a great writer. This conflicts him so much that he becomes suicidal; for the first time he is not just WONDERING if he wants to kill himself, but finds that he actually WANTS it (which in turn only adds to the conflict because being suicidal is something that makes him even MORE like on of the 'real' writers, and so it should make him HAPPY, right? What does he do???) So eventually he is walking down the train tracks daring God to send a train, to just end it (because—and here's the Sartre element I was waiting for—'WE'RE ALWAYS ENDING,' Patrick tells himself). So he's walking and screaming, 'It's not up to me!' and 'You do it!' And when the sun goes down and still no train has come it seems like a miracle, and he sits down on the tracks—at this point the actor has been pacing back and forth on the stage relating the story, and the stage directions say here that he sits down at the edge of the stage, letting his legs hang if the stage is an elevated stage—and he realizes no train came because he doesn't yet DESERVE to die. 'It was like God was speaking to me,' Simon writes for Patrick, 'I didn't deserve to die, and I didn't deserve to be happy. I had to earn both.' The here say that the lights change and the next scene starts almost seamlessly—the sister Claire walks into Patrick's bedroom where he has just delivered the monologue, and calls him into the apartment common room for breakfast. There he finds the Christmas tree artist from the night before coming out of the bathroom. It's clear his sister has slept with the guy, and the three of them sit there that Wednesday morning around the breakfast table before leaving for their different jobs. It's just the three of them, the only three characters in the play, really, at least the only ones that seem to have a real narrative behind them (and even that is loose at best, Simon really makes the audience work)—and the play ends with one of them saying, I forget which one says it, 'I hope things get better now.' It's only then that you remember that, oh yeah, this is election day, and you remember that feeling of HOPE everyone had the day Barack Obama became the President-Elect of the United States. It was a HOPE that went worldwide. Remember that, Spivey? At the table in the play it's sort of like that—the other two characters nod, and I remember it's the sister who says, 'I hope things get better,' and then the last character says, 'Yeah,' and that's it. There's a fade to black. It's a lovely ending, I think, because they're not happy, but they really believe that they will be, and we as the audience believe they will be, even though logically it doesn't make sense. But despite the dead parents and the dead babies (Claire mentions an abortion at one point, forgot to mention that a couple days ago when I telling you about Act One) and the thoughts of suicide and the idea of 'deserving' to die, in the end there's still that sense of hope. And hope, really, is a good thing. Hope is the only thing that makes us do anything, and doing something is the only way to happiness.*

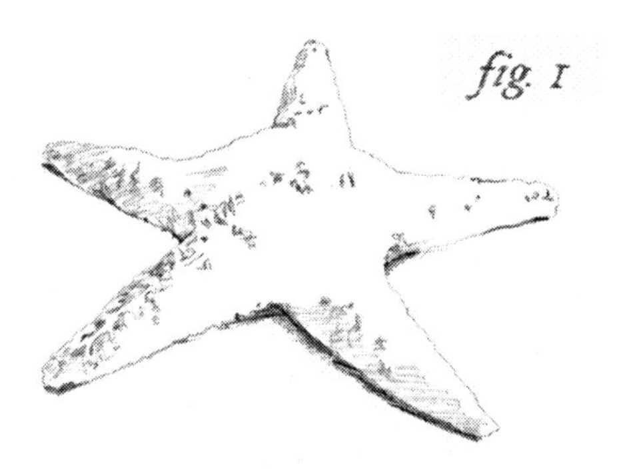

I'm twenty-eight years old when I leave Chicago to live with my grandmother in Ellensburg. Hers is a small house, in the middle of a small town, in the middle of Central Washington. I'd been a graduate student at DePaul, after I'd gotten the starfish and moved home from Asheville. I was out of money and had to leave. In Chicago I worked at a bar, tried to move on with things. Then I got pregnant. I told my mom as soon as I found out because I didn't know what else to do. She and my stepfather demanded I keep it. Put it up for adoption, they said, there was no way I could raise it. That was fine. The baby's father, I told him, but I wanted to have nothing to do with him, and for him to have no part in it. That was fine too. I took a leave of absence from school, told my advisor it was for personal reasons. Then one afternoon I was on the computer researching adoption agencies and I felt the sudden clutch on my chest, the burn of the starfish. I started bleeding and lost something in the toilet. I didn't look; the cramps hurt so bad I could imagine. I flushed because I didn't know what else to do.

Suddenly everything was supposed to be simpler. I was supposed to go back to being a graduate student. I said I wanted to take some time off. Everyone expected that. I was supposed to need some time. But after a few months of watching television on the couch my mother asked when I thought I would be ready to go back to school. I had been studying to be a teacher, something she loved being, but I decided I would leave Chicago, go live with my grandmother in Ellensburg. I visited once when I was a kid and remembered it being completely different than Chicago, the middle of nowhere when Chicago seemed the center of everywhere. I needed a change and so I left.

Now I take a partial load of classes at the college here. I'm working towards a master's degree in literature that should put me in a good place to be a teacher. When I get home from school my grandmother and I talk a bit about my day; she asks how I'm getting on, if I've made friends. We have those sorts of conversations. We make dinner together and I help her around the house with whatever she needs doing. She doesn't really need me. Not yet anyway. But I like being here. It's good for me to have a strong woman to look up to. She raised a family by herself after her husband died too young. That was in Olympia. She'd moved the family to Ellensburg afterwards, got a job doing the books for a produce company. She'd counted apples and cherries. She likes to say that. That she made sure everyone got his or her apples and cherries. My dad was her oldest and he left as soon as he could. Got a scholarship to a school in Indiana. Met my mom there.

It's autumn in Ellensburg, and the dry heat of summer has begun to make its natural rotation to a dry freeze. The Cascade Mountains separate Washington state into two distinct geographies and climates: moisture rolling in from the Pacific Ocean gets pierced by the peaks and releases onto the western half of the state, leaving the east dry as a desert, and the west green as a rainforest. Over time the two halves of Washington have evolved contrasting identities. Ellensburg is settled in the middle of the state, the simultaneous no-mans' and everyman's land, where cars traversing Interstate 90 between Seattle and Spokane will stop at one of our two interstate exits. After sharing the same counter for coffee and toast, drivers and passengers will be back on the road, back to their respective sides.

People who visit don't stay long, not long enough to be called tourists. And those who live here have their reasons, I guess. But these reasons do not include Ellensburg being their birthplace. Natives expatriate to urban centers elsewhere. Places like Chicago. Places like Seattle, like New York. Places where they can share in the identity of a specific history. Professional sports teams and city monuments.

That being said, I've been here six months now, and I'm enjoying myself.

The tiny bar I work in three nights a week is called Bloom's. It's about a mile from the university campus, but we don't get many students. It's too small and we don't serve food. My grandmother knew the place; not because she drinks but because she knows the owner from her days at the produce company. He lives about an hour away at Moses Lake and wanted someone to cover for him on the slower weeknights. I've only met him once, but he trusts my grandma and so I guess he trusts me. His name isn't Bloom, and I don't know where he got the name of the bar. I like to think it's because of James Joyce. But it's not an Irish place, so I don't know.

Bloom's isn't a dive, it's just small. It's very clean, too.

The regulars are from the neighborhood, mostly respectful old men who drink bottles of Budweiser or Bud Light and know my grandmother somehow, old produce workers and carpenters who each ended up in Ellensburg their own way. I like the older crowd; I like talking to them. From the conversations I've decided that the people who choose to live here don't do so for convenience. They do it for specific reasons, all of them. This is different than the high school kids who can't wait to leave, the natives like my father, who leave and marry elsewhere, eventually moving on again and leaving a mother and daughter to their own devices. These people leave Ellensburg to search for an identity outside of their own, to do something for themselves and find a sense of belonging to something larger, and it's something they never quite find. No one roots for sports teams here, there are no monuments and there is no skyline. No "Greetings from Ellensburg" postcards in the gas station convenience stores off the interstate. We like that here. We don't want to feel like they belong to something else. In fact if it weren't out of kindness to me these men would be just as content to drink at home. They could sip from their bottles of Bud and deal up fresh games of solitaire and mutter to themselves about the weather report. That's what they do in Bloom's.

Sometimes one of these men will say something that makes me think about the baby I might have had. And the baby's father, and I'll think then that it was a good thing I got pregnant. I met the father when I was working at a college bar in Lincoln Park. A place called Paddy O'Riley's. The owner there wasn't Irish and wasn't named Paddy or O'Riley, but the bar tried to be Irish like the name. So one night I poured my dead baby's father a cheap pint of bad Guinness and said hello. I had been trying to date, to meet someone who might do whatever needed to be done and usurp the memories of what happened in DC. It was over a year before I got pregnant. I wanted to love him—I can admit that. He was good to me, showed me men can be good. But the baby was what I needed; it made me comprehend that I was not—that I am not—ready to share my life with another person. Not completely. Not the way love is supposed to be. I remember lying in bed after I found out, thinking that the child inside me was going to be half him, half me. It was already mapped out genetically that way. It was fated. But where was the other half of me going to go? What was I giving up in this? I knew I was giving something up. I knew I had to get rid of the baby before it got here. I knew it was selfish. I know it was selfish. But we all deserve to be a little selfish now and again don't we? We can't be happy if we aren't a little selfish sometimes. It's impossible.

I still pretend not to have thought of names. For it.

One night I'm working at the bar. It's just Bob and me. Bob is an older man, a regular. He lives alone next door to my grandma, has dinner with us some nights. He did the yard work for my grandmother before I moved here. He still helps with the hard things, the things I resent a man having to do for us because we can't quite lift something. Some nights he'll give me a ride to Bloom's, and he'll sit with me through my shift shuffling cards and sniffing and wiping his gray mustache. He'll drink one beer when we sit down and then mugs of instant coffee until close. If the TV reception is bad he'll read one of his old paperback war novels he gets from the public library. We talk, but we're usually content to just do our own thing if business is slow. I'll read novels for school and he'll read his paperbacks and play his solitaire. Besides my grandmother, Bob is my best friend. I like that. He's probably her best friend, too. He worked with her for a couple years before she retired, driving trucks full of her apples and cherries to either side of the mountains. He's retired now, too. In the summer he likes to go barefoot, everywhere. I like that bit about him too, like he's an old hippy—even though he would hate being called a hippy.

Bob is on his first instant coffee when a woman walks in the door, someone neither of us recognize. She's 50 or 60. Not old, but not young either. Her hair is a blondish gray. It's hard to tell if it's more blonde or gray. She comes in alone, dressed like she's going to Sunday morning church, in a long fur coat and carrying probably her nicest purse and even wearing a hat with a ribbon. I say hello. She nods hello in return, and then asks for a gin martini with two olives. While I'm shaking the mixer I laugh and tell her I haven't had someone order a martini in this place, not ever probably. I look at Bob and he chuckles. The woman doesn't say anything, just sits down still wearing the coat and watches me make the drink. She takes the hat off and sets it on the stool next to her. She brushes the stool with her hand first, like it's dusty. She holds her purse in her lap. When I'm done I set it the glass on a coaster, pierce two green olives with a toothpick, drop them in the drink. I shrug my shoulders and look at her. I tell her it'll be five dollars, and she opens the fancy purse and pulls out this old antique-looking revolver pistol.

I back up. Lift my hands out to my sides. I am laughing, a bit out of fear and a bit just from the absurdity of the situation, and I ask if she's robbing me. But she just sets the gun on the bar like I'm not even there, its barrel leaning in my direction. Bob sits at the end of the bar watching, not moving. The TV seems loud in the silence, its newscast and poor reception just a terrible buzzing. But the woman, she just reaches back into her purse for a small wallet. Pulls out a five and a one. She hands them to me, and picks up her drink. She leaves the gun sitting there, sets her purse on the bar next to it. I step to the side, further away from the direction the gun's pointing.

"Jesus, honey, whatchu doin with that pistol in here?" Bob calls from down the bar. "That old gun don't even have a safety."

The woman sips her drink and doesn't reply. She's not dangerous, I think, just crazy. Maybe she was taking the gun to someone? Maybe her husband was a collector? I don't know. She's wearing a big, old wedding ring. I wonder if I should take the gun away from her. I don't want it to go off.

"I said that's dangerous!" Bob says, louder this time. He gets up, honestly concerned, and walks down the bar sniffing and wiping at his gray mustache. "That's god-damned stupid to be carryin 'round a gun with no safety!" He waves his arms in the air, trying to get her to look at him. "They call it a safety because it aint fuckin safe not to have it! Is it loaded? I sure hope you aint bringin a loaded gun with no safety into this place!"

"Please leave me alone, sir," the woman answers in a flat voice. She holds the martini at her lips, sipping tiny sips, while Bob stands over her in bewilderment. He reaches past her and picks up the gun. She doesn't stop him. He examines it and sets it back down. "It aint loaded," he tells me. I'm relieved. Then he says to the woman, "I'm mighty glad that aint loaded."

"Please leave me alone, sir," she says again, in the same flattened tone.

"Yeah, I'll leave you alone, sure." He looks at me. "I'm just tellin her, that aint safe. That aint safe carrying around something like that."

Bob goes back to his seat and sits, and the woman drinks her drink. I don't want to be rude by going to the other end of the bar and so I stand in the middle, equidistant between them, and away from the gun. Even if it's not loaded. I flip through channels on the TV and leave them both alone. I think about the woman though. What the hell was she was planning on doing with that gun? It was just fucking crazy, her having that old pistol. It's not like you need protection out here like you would in a city.

"Want another?" I call over when I see she's almost done. She's drunk it fast, and I'm glad.

"No. Thank you. I only wanted one."

"Something else?"

She shakes her head, brings her purse to her lap and rests her hands on top. "My husband's dead," she says. "He'd make these. I tried to make it at home but couldn't get it right."

I glance at Bob. A game of solitaire is laid out before him on the bar. But his hands are still. He's listening. I look back at the woman. "Oh," I say. "I'm sorry."

She holds the bag tight to her chest and stares at the gun. Probably came here to think about her husband, I think. And suddenly I am thinking about my baby's father. But I push him out of my head and start thinking about this poor lady instead, how she must live all alone, how she puts her best clothes on just to go outside and get a drink. She does all that just to think about her dead husband. Carries some old antique of his as a talisman. I think about that and don't let myself think about my baby or the toilet flush or the baby's father, who I was not going to mention again.

"How long has he been gone," I ask the woman. "Your husband."

"Not long, not long," she says. She picks up the gun and puts it in her bag, as if realizing how strange it was to leave it on the bar. "He said it made him feel important, to drink a drink like that. I just wanted to try one for once."

I don't know why she feels like she needs to explain herself. She seems so uncomfortable. I just want to make her comfortable, to focus on her and keep me comfortable, and so I ask if she's sure she doesn't want anything else. "I can make tea," I say. "If you don't like the martini. I can make you an Earl Gray. Or I think I have some chamomile." She starts to get up and looks me in the eyes for the first time. She smiles a weak and fake smile that scares me more than the gun did. "Thank you very much for making me his drink, young lady" she says. "It smelled just like his did."

She rises, walks toward the door.

"I'm sorry about your husband," I whisper after, but there's no way she heard it. The door swings shut.

"That his gun, you think?" Bob asks, walking down the bar as fast as I've ever seen him move. "The husband's? You think that's his gun?"

"I don't know," I say. "I don't...I don't know."

I turn away and start moving bottles around, tidying up the bar. Bob stands where he is for a moment and I see him in the reflection off the bottles as he goes and sits back down at his seat. That poor lady, I think. That poor lady. She's like my nightmare. It probably was her husband's gun, just something of his. I don't ever want to be in a situation where my life is so dependent on another that I don't have anything left when the other dies. That's why people live in places like this, these towns that are just two exits on an interstate. It's to preserve their own identity. To not become a New Yorker or a Bostonian or a Seattleite. That's why the men that come to Bloom's would be just as happy to drink at home. They come to be nice to me. They think that because I'm here from Chicago that I can't be left alone. But I would be fine alone, just like them. That woman had never tasted her husband's drink, didn't know what it was that made him feel important. She only knew what it smelled like. Now that he's gone she has to come to me to make her one. Maybe she brought the gun to protect herself from his ghost.

I tell Bob I'll be right back and I throw on an old Carhartt jacket someone left the other night and go outside to find the woman. It's below freezing for the first time since I moved here and the air smells like winter. I can see my breath, and through the mist I can make out the woman's fur-coated and ribbon-hatted silhouette down the empty street. She gets into an old truck parked on the gravel shoulder across from Bob's truck. Her dead husband's truck.

I call out and run after her but the red brake lights flash and the truck starts and it's gone before I get to it. I watch it go, and then walk back.

Bob is behind the bar pouring hot water for his instant coffee. I tell him she drove off in a big truck I didn't recognize.

"Maybe she killed him," he says. "She killed the husband by accident — but not really by accident — during dinner tonight and came in for a drink, his drink, just to spite the fucker. He was foolin' 'round on her. Now she's stole his truck and's trying to get outta town before the neighbors can smell him. Waddya think?" He's smiling. He knows why I moved to Ellensburg, what happened. He can tell I'm thinking about it, and he's trying to make me feel better by making a joke. Can't blame him. It's worked before. But I can't help wondering what the woman's name was.

"I don't know," I say in a flat tone, and start washing the martini glass. We only have four martini glasses, and I need to be careful.

"It's possible," Bob says, trying to get a rise out of me. I stay quiet, wiping the glass in the dishwater with a pink sponge. We only have four of the glasses. Have to be careful. They're delicate, very delicate. Can't break one. If I break one that will mean I'm bad at this job. And I need this job.

Bob watches me, leaves me to my glass. He goes back to his solitaire and his seat.

I wash for a few minutes. Then I set the very clean martini glass down and look up at him. "Hey Bob," I say. "How old are you?"

He looks up from his solitaire game. "I'm sixty-three," he says.

"You ever been married?"

"Why? You lookin?" He smiles.

"No, just wondering." I smile back at him. The smile feels fake and weak, but it's still a smile. "I feel rude for having known you this long and not knowing if you were ever married."

He chuckles and leans forward. His elbows rest on the bar. "Yeah, I was married," he says. "Don't much talk about it. A long time ago, not for very long. Said she didn't love me anymore, so she left. I was always driving. Back and forth across the mountains, not here much. I don't blame her. You can't love something that isn't there, I guess. Guess it was easier for me to be alone than it was for her."

I nod and pick the martini glass back up and wipe it dry with a hand towel. Bob turns the TV to the news. It's poor reception, the newscasters' faces all grainy. They're giving sports scores.

"Missed the weather," he says, and clicks it off. He looks at me with concern. "Well kiddo, you wanna head out a bit early tonight? No one's comin' in on a cold one like this. No one's gonna care if you close early. Your boss is way off in Spokane this week anyway, he won't know."

"Yeah," I say. "Sure." I set the martini glass with its three dusty counterparts on the shelf behind the bar. "I hope that woman's okay."

"I was just thinking that, too," Bob says. We're both quiet for a moment. Bob puts his cards in his pocket and walks around to my side of the bar with his coffee mug. He hesitates a little, but pats my shoulder twice. He rinses the mug out in the dishwater and releases the drain. I get my coat.

A couple minutes later I lock up and we're walking down the empty street. There's no trace left of the woman or her truck. I look at my breath as it comes out of me. I try to make it like smoke rings but can't. That doesn't work with breath.

"Winter's comin," Bob starts saying. "That's why I'm a little bothered. Why I cursed at that woman. I'm sorry about that, by the way. I'm just nervous about the winter. You can feel it, when yer a driver. The mountains get all white, covered in ice an' snow, beautiful. But you live or die on the report of which pass is open when yer a driver. Every year you look at the mountains and think, 'Now that's fuckin beautiful. God made that beautiful. But someone's gonna die up there in the next few months. Jus gonna slip, some unlucky fool, to their death.'"

We get to the truck and he unlocks the passenger side and holds the door open for me. This kind old man. I think about his wife, how she left him, why she left him.

"Well I'm just glad that woman's in a big truck, that's all I'm sayin," Bob says, as he climbs in on the driver side and starts his own truck. We've only got a half mile to go but he turns the heat on anyway. For me. This kind old man. "I'm just glad she's got somethin safe to get her to where she's goin," he says. "That's all."

I look out the window into the dark where I know the mountains rise out of the ground, even though I can't see them. Bob looks over at me as he shifts into second gear. "Whaddya thinking about, kiddo?"

"Nothing," I say, but I know how much money I have, and that I need to go somewhere else now. I think about Asheville, and the man on fire, and I think: I was strong there.

Richard Hugo poems were drifting through his head. A stanza about a love beginning; a line about a beer can. In the distance the Olympic Mountains glowed, backlit by a phosphorus moon that reflected in the nighttime water of Puget Sound like a great white fish. Martin lit a cigarette, leaned against the balcony railing on the 14th floor of his downtown hotel. There had been a gun in his dream. A bright, gleaming gun, beautiful in metal and silver. Only when he'd realized it was pointed at him did he wake. He'd swung his legs out from under the tight sheets of the Westin bed and walked across the hard carpet in his boxers. The red digital had glowed 2:45, blinking, which he'd thought was strange. He had pulled aside the drapes to the sliding door and had stepped outside. The wind had chilled off Elliott Bay and given him goosebumps on his thighs. He'd gone back inside and put on the suit jacket hanging from the typical hotel chair, and in the breast pocket he'd found a thin box of Nat Sherman cigarettes brought from Manhattan and a Seattle Mariners lighter bought that morning at the airport. Back on the balcony he lit one of the black cigarettes, leaned forward on the black railing. Then he reflected on all that had just happened, as if watching a recording of himself: 2:45 AM, black night, black water, smoking a black cigarette on a dark balcony, and he thought of Richard Hugo. He watched a single car drive through the yellow-orange glow of the street below, heading south past the base of the black Columbia Tower that rose tallest of the metropolitan skyline. Staring at the black-on-black silhouette he smoked and thought. Across the bay he could see the faint outline of Alki Beach where the first white-skinned settlers of the Denny Party came and made camp in the region a century-and-a-half ago. They called it New York-Alki, the word 'alki' meaning 'by and by' or 'with time' to the brown-skinned natives. What their dreams must have been like, Martin thought, letting black ash flutter to the street. White pioneers came to a calm blue bay and watched a future metropolis rise in their imaginations like giant glass flowers sprouting from the earth. A new New York, blossoming from their hard work, from their white Christian American dreams. Martin thought of the Denny Party and he thought of Hugo's poem "Alki Beach," the poem in which he wrote of a love beginning and ending on that beach, of bubbles disappearing in the surf, of a beer can rolling and floating in the rocks. Sleeping somewhere in that neighborhood was Martin's high school friend Greg, with his new wife Madeleine. The wedding was the reason Martin flew home to the Pacific Northwest for the long weekend. What family Martin had left was still in Olympia, a little over an hour to the south. He would drive there in the morning for lunch and a visit, and then return the rental car at Sea-Tac Airport and catch the red eye back to JFK. It would be early morning in New York when he arrived, as if he had slept through the night and this trip had only been a dream. Martin turned from the railing and leaned back, facing the hotel room. He held the cigarette in his mouth and rubbed his cold thighs with both hands. He imagined the railing breaking beneath his weight and imagined the terror of a fall, the loss of balance, the rollercoaster feeling in the stomach, the realization of what was happening. He felt a real rush of adrenaline and moved away. They say it's not the ground that kills you but the cardiac arrest on the way down. He took a deep breath and listened to the silence. Claire hadn't come with him. His grandmother would want to know about that, and he'd have to say it was because of the baby. Again, because of Anna, and his grandmother would tell him to put his trust in God, to trust that what had happened to Anna was the right thing to have happened. A year and a half ago Martin and Claire had gotten married (they were still married, in truth) and eight months ago Anna, the baby, had died. It was nobody's fault. She was born early. She was without oxygen for several minutes in the birth canal, her tiny body tangled in the umbilical cord. What bit of luck and air she needed wasn't there. 16 days in a special part of the hospital, surrounded by the smell of sterility and cold electronics. 16 days of Martin and Claire living in the hospital and staring at what was supposed to be their daughter. A strange and tiny, unclassifiable creature. Something about her seemed unreal, despite her tangible presence in the box. Like a seahorse, in a box like an aquarium. During that time Martin had hoped the girl would die. He didn't pray—no, he couldn't pray—but he had hoped. She would be born with mental problems, the doctors had said, how much impairment, we don't know, they said, but you should prepare yourself for that. If she survives, they said, there's a good chance she will be retarded. Martin wasn't proud of it, but he had hoped for death. So they could try again and get it right. God might have been saying: Thanks for playing, better luck next time. The anticipation of

Anna had given Claire and him expectations that were not met, and maybe, Martin had thought, maybe they would do better on a second try. For 16 days he kept picturing variations on a stereotype: a daughter that wore diapers forever, that couldn't read, that couldn't talk right. Half of both Claire and Martin went into this thing in the box, she was what their love and DNA hath wrought. And so when Anna finally did die, when Martin told the doctors, That's enough, because Claire couldn't or wouldn't say those words, Anna died broken and strange in the middle of tubes and wires and beeps and hisses. Claire and Martin's remaining halves sank to the bottom of a great mass of blame and hurt and shit. Whose half had fucked up? Whose was the more broken half? They had not separated yet, but it had been almost a year. They would not last another, Martin was sure. They both carried shit and brokenness inside them now, and it was not unreasonable, Martin thought, leaning over the balcony edge again and watching smoke float into the sky above Fourth Avenue, for the solution to be his own running home, to come back to the Northwest and toss whatever he remembered of Anna and Claire off Alki Beach like an old beer can. He could stare off from the Point at the end of West Seattle like those first settlers, and like Richard Hugo he could imagine a new love beginning, his old love just a dented can of Rainier against the rocks. Claire could and would continue to blame him for Anna after he'd gone, that would be her right, and his role in her life would be like a cancer, stealing six years with this relationship. That would have to be okay. Martin stubbed the last of the cigarette out beside him on the railing and realized he was terrified to divorce, to acknowledge with words and signatures that when Anna died, they died too. But it was the right thing, the best thing. He stood there for a moment and then stepped fast inside the hotel room for the bottle of champagne he'd been given as part of the wedding party's rehearsal dinner the night before. He unwrapped it of its golden tissues and carried it out to the balcony. He held it up to the moonlight and read the French label that meant nothing to him. A toast, he thought, a toast is in order. Yes, this is the right thing to do, to start this new life. He lit another cigarette and held it in his mouth as he untwisted the cork and, shaking the bottle, shot the cork with a blast across the avenue. White foam spilled out over his suit jacket and bare legs. He dropped the cigarette from his mouth and the orange tip burned his foot. He swore, and not knowing what else to do, threw the bottle out toward the bay where it fell like a dying seagull onto the empty street, its half-empty guts foamy and white on the pavement after a faint noise. Martin let himself fall against the wall separating his balcony from the one next door and sat in the puddle of champagne foam. He would miss her. But he was exhausted from missing what might have been, the dreams that were supposed to become real, that he and Claire had together when she was pregnant, dreams of them and the unborn Anna as a family, as a home. He was glad the baby hadn't lived, but he wished more that it had never been a possibility, that he and Claire could have just gone back to what small home they'd created together before she'd gotten pregnant. Home had seemed more a verb than a noun, something they would do together, as a family, not something that could be given and taken as it had been with Anna. Anna is a challenge from God, Martin's grandmother had told him on the phone during those 16 days. A challenge you are going to have to accept. No one is in control of one's own life, as much as you might think it feels like you are. God chooses for you. God is in control. You need to be at home in God, Martin. Martin had thought then what he whispered to himself on the balcony, a quiet curse to God. He leaned his head back against the wall, retrieved the box of Nat Shermans from his pocket and lit a new one, setting the box back on the railing above his head. There had been another story his grandmother told him. He had thought about it a lot during the hours sitting next to Anna in her seahorse-aquarium-box. She told Martin one evening about a dream she kept having in the days before she got word his grandfather had been shot in the leg and would be coming home. She'd said she felt so lonely in Ellensburg. She'd cry at night, and it was worse when she hadn't heard from him for a time. Weeks passed between the moment he was shot and the notice saying that he would be home soon. She kept having the same dream: Martin's grandfather driving down their street in Ellensburg as she sat at the window watching him approach in his old cherry red Ford pick-up. She would wave and he would wave back, but as soon as that happened hundreds of Axis soldiers would appear behind him in tanks and camouflaged jeeps with mounted machine guns. They would be gaining fast, shooting and screaming German and Italian curses she couldn't understand but knew were curses, to her and him and the God that wanted them to be together. Explosions and gunshots would rattle in her head. She would be standing in the window screaming at her husband to Hurry! Hurry! And then he'd have a gun in his hand too and would be shooting out the back window of the pickup, back at the soldiers, and he would scream to her that he was Coming! I'm coming!—and suddenly it would all stop, and he was just there, standing in front of the window on the front porch, and the street would be all empty and quiet behind them, and she would stand there and look at her husband, home, finally, after so long, and she told Martin that every time she had the dream it would end with her looking at him through the window and saying, Oh thank God you're home! Oh thank God my husband is home! and Martin's grandfather would just smile and look over her shoulder through the window that separated them, and he would see the house she'd lived in with the Finnish cousins the past two years, he would see that she had started a life in America without him, was part of a family already, this family he didn't recognize. And he would stop smiling, look deep into her happy and God-thanking tearful eyes, and put the gun to his chest and shoot himself right through the heart—before she'd be able to open the door. It was her guilt, she told Martin, it was her guilt that she had started life without him that convinced her to leave Ellensburg and take her war-torn husband to Seattle. He returned safe in a wheelchair, delivered like a parcel, unaccompanied by gunfire or chase, and she left the Finnish cousins she'd loved for two years. I felt like I had stolen two years of happiness from him, she'd said. He had years stolen by the war, but then he had to come back and see that during those two years I'd become an American, had learned what to eat and how to act. He was two years behind me. Decades later and his grandfather dead, Martin sat in a puddle of champagne, in the middle of the cold night in downtown Seattle, and he thought about Claire and the six years they'd been together. He rationalized. Yes, it was the same thing. If he left her and she met someone else it would be like he had stolen six years of potential happiness she could have had with that other man. The only thing to do now was for Martin to leave, to run home. I had stolen two years from him, his grandmother had said, but on the other side of the mountains we could start a new life and put our trust in God. Martin stubbed his cigarette out in the champagne-y foam. His throat was raw, and he wondered if Claire would meet someone else, if he would ever meet someone else, and he didn't care either way. Then he hoped Claire would. Several minutes passed and he thought of nothing but the good times between Claire and him—the vacations to different European cities, the holidays, the anniversaries—and he tried to think about what she must imagine he owed her still. They had just come to their logical conclusion now. Maybe she knew it too. He threw the soaked cigarette over the edge of the railing and pulled himself up and went inside. He walked across the room and pulled off his wet boxers and jacket and climbed into bed naked. He lay there for a while but still couldn't sleep, his thoughts like hot champagne in his head. He lay there and thought how these thoughts he was thinking, if they weren't God—and he didn't believe they were—then they must be just the chemical reactions between enzymes and neurons and other scientific things he didn't know the names of. Antidepressants, drugs—they could change the way the chemicals burn and give him different thoughts. How he felt about Claire, there were drugs that could change that. Certain combinations of synaptic firings that could make his body feel a certain thing. Like reflexes. Exactly like reflexes, he thought. And God. Belief in God. What would his childhood priest have said to him? If belief in God is just electricity in the brain, just an illusion, Martin's priest would have said, then you have to ask yourself, Marty, who controls the switch? If you are telling me that God is just a symptom of something we can't understand, because our thoughts are controlled by the very thing we're trying to think about, well then I tell you that it is Faith that tells me God is the 'controller,' God is what Descartes hypothesized as the evil daemon that might make everything we see or think a delusion. Whatever it is that makes you and I think, that enables you and me to know the difference between right and wrong, that is God, Marty. You can rationalize whatever you want about Anna, but Faith will always triumph over rationalization. That's what his priest would say, perhaps. His argument would rest on the Catholic Faith as a fulcrum, and Martin would want to ask then, Can't God create Faith then, by your definition? Martin tried to imagine what his priest would say to that, but that thought yielded silence, nothing, and he wondered what it was that let him imagine those answers from his priest in the first place. He lay in bed and thought until the sun came up. Then he climbed out of bed, pulled on his damp boxers, and walked back out onto the balcony to watch the dawn ferries crossing the water. He stared west at the sun breaking out from behind the mountains—and he felt warm, and he knew then that wanted to believe in God, and he didn't care if it was in fact God that was making him want that or not, if it was or wasn't Faith. It was just what he wanted to do, to believe. To let go and feel no adrenaline or fear. He wanted to believe he wasn't in control. He wanted to believe he needed to come back here, to start over and call this home. He could forget Anna and Claire and let that just be the past; he could believe those years were stolen from him just as much as they were from Claire. He saw the pack of cigarettes on the railing and crumpled them in his fist. In his new life he would be a non-smoker, he decided. In the distance a ferry gave off a low-pitched blast from its horn as it passed in front of Alki Beach. It was true that the first settlers from the East came to Seattle and named it New York-Alki. But then the name was changed to honor the chief of the natives, albeit misspelled. *Sealth,* the chief had been called. Martin watched the ferries and thought back to the Richard Hugo poem, and to the poet lingering in the melancholy of those forgotten settlers: "Where whites first landed / is forgotten" he wrote. A love began on that beach, between those who first landed and their new home. A love began, and then years later a poet in a long dark coat walked along the shore and saw a beer can rolling alone and untended in the surf. And the poet thought about things. Martin stood on the balcony and breathed in deep the salt air. Tomorrow he would go back to New York. He stood there on the balcony in a puddle of champagne and he thought about his future. About happiness, and the things he would do now, and what he would write.

fig. 3

The doc looks at the file in her hand, then up at me sitting across from her in the uncomfortable yellow chair. So Eddie, she says, I understand your sister visited last week. Step-sister, I say. Step-sister, right, the doc corrects herself. Sorry, I read that wrong. That's alright, I say. The doc sets the file down on her desk and leans back. Are you two close? she asks, but I'm looking past her now, through the window where I can see it's starting to rain, and I can see young soldiers doing jumping-jacks in tiny formation at Fort Lewis across the highway. I could have been one of them, I think. I could have been one of them, not me, sitting here. You and your sister, the doc asks again, Are you close? I look away from the soldiers. I think so, I say. S understands me. S is what you call her? I nod. Why did you correct me to say she was your step-sister? I shrug. I don't know, I say. Just wanted to be correct is all. The doc shifts her weight and her chair creaks. I don't know why it creaks, because I'm pretty sure it's more comfortable than mine; mine is cold, and I'm only wearing a t-shirt and pajama bottoms so I'm freezing. Can you tell me about your family? the doc asks. What do you want to know that isn't in that file already? I say. Tell me some more about your step-sister, S. Tell me, for instance, when did she become your step-sister? We have the same step-father, I say, He must have told you; you must know what happened with my mom. Okay, the doc says, yes, I know a lot. But I want to hear your perspective on things. Tell me what happened with the half-brother you've mentioned, tell me what happened with—she checks her file—Robbie.

The opening of *Anna Karenina*, I say. Happy families are all alike. That's how Tolstoy starts. Then he clarifies that unhappy families find unhappiness in their own ways. So it's immediately set up, you see, Tolstoy establishes right away that the unhappy family is the more interesting family. It's true, of course, especially for a novel it's true, and now, talking about the whole thing, I—I don't know. I guess my family is more interesting too. My step-sister is probably my closest family even though I don't know if I would call us close. Not as close as step-siblings in a happy family, at least. But yeah, you asked about Robbie—and from my point of view, like you said, which is good, because I don't really care what Roger has to say about what happened. The fucker wasn't there and I don't feel like I have to justify myself to him. But when I was 18 I was living with him, Robbie, and my mom in Everett. My real dad had run off when I was five or six and my mom remarried to Roger when I was seven or eight. She had Robbie about three years after that. Roger worked on the assembly floor at Boeing and my mom was my middle school English teacher. Even after they got married I was still closer to my mom than he was. It wasn't a total Oedipal complex like you're thinking, though. I used to think that the only thing Roger could give my mom that I couldn't was a dick to fuck, so I can tell you it wasn't what you might be thinking. But then, after my mom died, I went ahead and told Roger that all he ever was to her was just a dick for her to fuck, and he hit me and I hit him back and broke his nose and part of his cheekbone and we haven't talked since. That was in Chicago, a few weeks after she died, when I was left with just step- and half- relatives. I'm sure this is all in the file but I'll tell you again. So the night before the Robbie thing happened I'd been out late and slept at a friend's. When I got home in the morning my mother was supposed to be asleep still, and I sat eating Cheerios in the kitchen and reading the paper. Then Robbie came in with a bucket full of garter snakes he'd caught in the backyard. I didn't even think about where he was supposed to have been. It was summer vacation and he was going to a day camp, soccer or basketball at the rec center. I must have figured he was at camp or something, I don't know, but I remember we'd just moved into that house and there were boxes still all over the place. Some pictures were on the walls, a big cuckoo clock. A few months earlier my mom and I had walked through the house together, when it was still only framing, because she had wanted to show it to me alone, without Roger and Robbie, and that way we could talk about it. I remember she had pointed at different corners and chalked outlines on plywood, saying things like, This will be the kitchen, this will be the dining room, etcetera, taking me through what were still just ideas of kitchens and dining rooms. I'd done my best to imagine the 2 x 4's as painted white walls like she was doing—family photos hanging, bookshelves leaning, all that. And I'd checked the guts of plumbing and wiring between the studs like I knew what they were, all the black and red tangles that would be hidden away once the house was finished. I remember she showed me where the sliding door out to the backyard would be, and I remember her being really excited about the view of the mountain. I remember the word WEYERHAESER was stenciled everywhere in green spray paint like tattoos. I kept thinking about how much wood it took to make a house. Even then I could recognize that she needed me to love it, that I absolutely *had* to love it. Because for her it sort of represented the family she'd been trying to hold together ever since my real dad left. That was how she loved me then, once she'd had another son, with another husband. I think she thought it made her a bad mother, having done it all over again. Like she thought of her first attempt at family a failure. I can see what her logic was: that if the first family was one of unhappiness, then by trying again and doing everything completely differently the second time, then the second family would have to be a happy one, perfectly normal like all the other happy families out there. Of course it doesn't work like that, Aristotelian logic doesn't take into account something as unmathematical and unsure as daily life. But I tried my best to understand what she wanted and I tried my best to be the son that she wanted. I remember I walked outside to where the backyard would be, down a piece of lumber that served as a ramp. Empty lots stretched out to distant trees, and the construction equipment seemed like tanks positioned across a no-man's land. It was like Desert Storm, but with a light rain, and Mt. Rainier was like this magnificent inverse mushroom cloud. She watched me and said, Lots of neighbors. Meaning it as a good thing. Cigarettes butts were scattered across the dirt, and I remember thinking the filters looked like infantry for the construction equipment artillery. Roger, he smoked. I would steal cigarettes from his jacket pocket once or twice a week. He never said anything but I'm sure he knew. He has cancer now too, S says. Anyway, I was just about Robbie's age when my mother remarried to him, but still just old enough to know that I would be willing to kill Roger to protect her, even if maybe I wasn't strong enough then. Telling him that when I was seven years old would have been cute. 'I'll kill you if you hurt my mom,' says the little boy. But if I'd said it later, when I was eighteen, it would have been essentially the same thing as when I told him he wasn't anything but a dick to be fucked, which, yeah, I did, but later. But yeah, before my mom died, before that we got along okay. Mostly it was just each of us respecting that my mother wanted the other one in her life, and that was enough. And he was a nice enough guy. When my mom suggested getting a house in the new development he hadn't batted an eye, and he bought it just because my mother loved it. So he certainly wasn't a bad man. Walking back up the ramp into what would be the kitchen, I remember my mom just watching me, wondering what I was going to say, waiting for me to do something. Roger's a good guy for getting you this house, I told her, and she corrected me that he was getting *us* this house. It's *our* house, she said. *Our family's* house, and I nodded and just kept looking around, and then after making her wait a bit longer I told her that I liked it, and asked if Roger liked it, and she just said, Oh you know Roger, waving her arm around. It seemed like something was bothering her, and even then I wondered if something was wrong between them, but I didn't say anything because I didn't want to ruin the house for her. She was playing with some of the wires weaving through the studs, and I said: I'm guessing you like it though, right mom? and I remember she smiled huge and got so excited and started talking really fast, saying, Oh I love it! You just, you just have to imagine it done. They have a house, near the gate, one that's all furnished and clean. And it's just beautiful inside! Not the same layout as this exactly, but you get the idea, and she stood there and looked around at the empty room, imagining it full, chalk outlines on the floor growing into future appliances, invisible doors opening to reveal elaborate Gatsby-esque parties full of gay Daisys and Toms. She seemed so happy and I was glad for her, and I walked over and put an arm around her shoulder. I remember she leaned into my chest and grabbed my arm and whispered, Such a strong boy. We stayed like that for a while before she squeezed my arm once more and said we should go because Roger and Robbie would be home soon, and we drove back to the house across town. A couple months later I was in that same kitchen with all the walls done and some pictures and a cuckoo clock hung and all that red and black wiring hidden away where it belonged, and I sat reading the newspaper, looked at the clock, and jumped to my feet to wake her. I got up and poured another cup of coffee for myself, and then, when I turned around, I found Robbie standing at the sliding door, a five gallon bucket in one hand and a black garter snake dangling like a length of rubber hose in the other. His too-big Mariners hat was flopped low on his forehead to cover his face like it always did then, so that he had to tilt his head back to look at anyone, and he yelled, Check it out, Eddie! and held up the snake. Now tell me this ain't the biggest garden snake you've ever seen! It's gar-*ter* snake, man, I corrected him, and told him to get out of there before mom caught him in the house with a snake, because she would have flipped her shit. But Robbie just held the snake by the tail and swung it back and forth like a pendulum, working at getting the snake's head to come as close to the glass door as possible without hitting it. I mean, I used to chase snakes like that when I was Robbie's age, too, in the old backyard in Renton before he was around, but I didn't torture them like that. I just liked how they felt, slithering between my fingers when my hand was spread wide. I was about to yell at him to stop fucking with the snake when he said, Mom's at the doctor, and I just watched the snake's tongue flickering in and out as he swung it. What do you mean she's at the doctor? I asked finally, but all he said was, Do you think snakes puke? I mean, if you get them dizzy enough? I couldn't blame him for not knowing what was happening but I yelled at him anyway. What the hell happened you little fuck! And that just stunned him. You said fuck, he whispered, but I could tell he thought it meant he had something on me now, and so I grabbed his arm and took the swinging snake out of his hand and tossed it into the yard, to show him he still needed to listen to me, you know, and I yelled at him to tell me what happened. But he really didn't know, just whined that he'd been watching TV when his dad came home and said he was taking mom to the hospital. He said his dad told him not to go outside but figured it would be okay because I never really cared what he did, whether he stayed inside or out. So I told him to go see if he couldn't find a bigger snake than that one and sent him jogging out, happy with his challenge. I remember watching him go before I dialed to make sure he couldn't hear, and I could see into the bucket still swinging in his hand where there were at least half a dozen more garter snakes slithering over and under each other like a bunch of tangled cords. Once he was out I dialed my mom's cell phone and it rang five times and then went to voicemail. I tried again, and even though I knew something was wrong, I knew that if something were *really* wrong, she would have called me. It hadn't been long after that first time she took me to see the house that we were sitting in her old Subaru station wagon in the Safeway parking lot and she told me how she'd been to the doctor and was going to need surgery. There was a mass in her colon, she'd said, and it was starting to spread and they needed to get at it right away. I remember she said, They stuck a camera up my ass, and she made a horrible sound somewhere between laughter and crying, this terrible cough-like sound. She kept saying, Can you believe it? I've got ass cancer. It was the only time I remember her swearing after my dad left, she was always careful with language. I made it all the way through shopping at the Safeway, even through her buying me my favorite frozen lasagna for dinner, but then when I looked over at her in the driver's seat on the way back I really realized what it meant for her to be sick like that. I know it sounds melodramatic but I told her that if she died I would kill myself, and I know I meant it when I said it, and she just put her hand on my leg and smiled and told me it would all be fine, it was early, they had caught it early, and that was something I would get used to telling myself again and again. But in any case I could see that she was crying too, and it wasn't just because her son was crying. Then, after Robbie went to bed that night, she and Roger asked me not to tell him. They told me I was older so I could handle it, I could understand it, and I had a right to know. Roger said that last part, and I could tell he hadn't wanted to tell either of us, either me or Robbie, but wanted to keep it as something just between him and my mom. I swear to god I don't know what would have happened if Roger had convinced her to keep it a secret. But Robbie didn't need to know anything other than that his mommy was sick, they said, and so I said okay, and over the next few months she had treatments and surgeries, and a week after we moved into the new house my mom went in for a big operation. Roger took Robbie fishing and I stayed and waited at the hospital. I remember smoking Roger's cigarettes outside the glass doors to pass the time, and nurses kept stopping to ask if I was okay, and I just kept waving them off and kept telling myself that it was still early, that they'd still caught it in time and everything would be okay and in a few hours the doctors would come and get me and tell me we could go back to being a perfectly normal and happy family.

I stop talking for a few moments. The doc sits and watches me. You okay, Eddie? she asks. Yeah, I say, just, you know, it's not something I talk about. Take all the time you want, she says, and I nod. My mom had never been very religious, I say after a while. I wonder about that sometimes. What do you mean? the doc asks. I wonder what happens to people who aren't religious when they die, I say. I mean, what goes through their heads? There must be a part of everyone that wants some kind of life to go on. My mom was raised Catholic, and she had me baptized but not confirmed, and since my real dad left I haven't been to a church hardly at all, except for her wedding to Roger and then her funeral, but I know she didn't really practice Catholicism, and she didn't really believe in Heaven or Hell. Me, I'm not sure what I believe in so I can't really wish one way or another, you know? I have a hard time believing that she's in Heaven and watching over me or whatever—but I do want to believe that. Not just because it's nice to think she's not really gone, but because it's even nicer to think that when *I* die I won't be gone either, it won't just be a simple ending of existence. Maybe I'll see her again, you know? I think if it were *me* dying, I think I'd pray, just as a way of hedging my bets at least, before I had to face whatever it is a person has to face. I think everyone must hope for *something*, and so you must do *something* in the hope that this isn't really all there is. Anyway. This is my long way of saying I wasn't there when she died. She died later the same day that Robbie came in with the snakes. Something had happened, a suture had come loose, I don't know, and she went back into the hospital and died there from a blood clot that went to her heart and killed it. So I sent Robbie back outside to look for more snakes and called my mom, who didn't answer, and then I tried Roger, who was supposed to be at work but who apparently had come home and taken my mom to the hospital, and he answered the phone and just said: Eddie, I can't talk right now, and told me my mom had had an accident, and I needed to keep Robbie out of the bedroom, or take him to a movie, or whatever. He'd left money on top of the fridge, he said. I remember I started to say something and the asshole cut me off, just saying: Do this for me, Edward, and hanging up. I called back and he didn't answer. I called again and again. Finally it went straight to voicemail, which meant he'd turned off his phone. So I threw the phone against the wall and ran up the stairs and to my mom's bedroom, threw open the door, and it was just solid stench. Bedding was everywhere but the bed, the stained mattress was uncovered, there was blood on the white sheets, a towel in the corner wrapped like a whip and soaked the color of beach sand. I just stood there in the doorway, breathing, listening, thinking. I remember thinking that this is what cancer smells like, like blood and shit and piss. Her cell phone was flipped open on the floor, with dark fingerprints on the numbers, and that's when I realized she had called Roger. She'd known I was at my friend's. It wouldn't have taken me more than five minutes, maybe ten to get back to the house. It would have taken Roger at least fifteen, twenty even, to get there from work. So I don't know why she called Roger instead. But I shut the door and it was like there was a fist in my throat. I walked down the stairs, found two twenties on top of the refrigerator and left them there. I remember imagining what must have happened. The sutures coming loose, the ripping, bleeding, diarrhea. I tried Roger's phone again but it was still voicemail. I started gagging and was throwing up in the sink when I heard Robbie come through the door again and he asked what was wrong. I was crying and my eyes hurt from throwing up and gagging but I still remember turning and seeing what that little bastard had done. He was standing there like he'd been before, with the bucket in one hand and a snake dangling in the other, but this time the snake was hanging limp and dead with its tongue drooping out. The little fuck had tied its body into a square knot. I remember the lower part of the body was thicker than the tail, from all the blood the knot had trapped. Then before I knew what I was doing I'd grabbed Robbie and thrown him outside onto the grass, and I had my knee in his chest and was punching him in the nose and eyes and jaw again and again as hard as I could. When I stopped, one of his front teeth was stuck in my hand, and I saw all the other garter snakes he'd caught slithering out of the bucket and across the new lawn like eels in green silk. A couple hours later my mom died. I'd called 911 when Robbie wouldn't wake up and they took us both to the same hospital. He had to have his jaw wired and I'd broken two of his ribs with my knee, but he was fine otherwise. I wasn't there when my mother died because I was in the back of a police car. Roger wasn't with her either, but was downstairs in the emergency room with Robbie. I don't know if there was even a nurse there. I wish there had at least been a nurse, so my mom could have told someone what was going through her head, so she could have told someone that she loved me, and that I'd meant more to her than Roger, and that she wished she'd called me instead. If she had called me instead it would have meant I'd been sitting with her when she died, and she wouldn't have had to go through it alone.

The doc sighs. You know, Eddie, she says, opening her file again and leaning forward with a pen in her hand. I don't think you're a bad person, not a bad person at all. She looks me in the eye. Thanks, I say. But that story you just told me, she goes on, ignoring me, That story about how much you loved your mother? How you wished you could have been there? That's not what it says here at all. It wasn't Robbie you did that to. And it wasn't Roger, either. She taps the pen against her desk. Yeah, I say. I know. You were there in the hospital when she died, weren't you, she says. We both sit there quietly for a few moments, and I don't say anything. One of my knees starts to bounce up and down. I rub my arms to keep from getting cold. I guess maybe Tolstoy would say that unhappy people remember unhappiness in their own ways, I say finally. And I get up and try to walk out of the room, but the orderly grabs me and forces me to sit back down. I make cold fists with my hands. Now, the doc says, Let's start again.

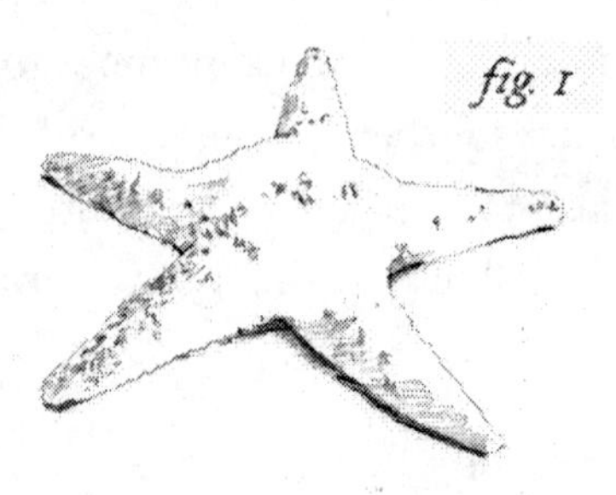

fig. 1

fig. 2

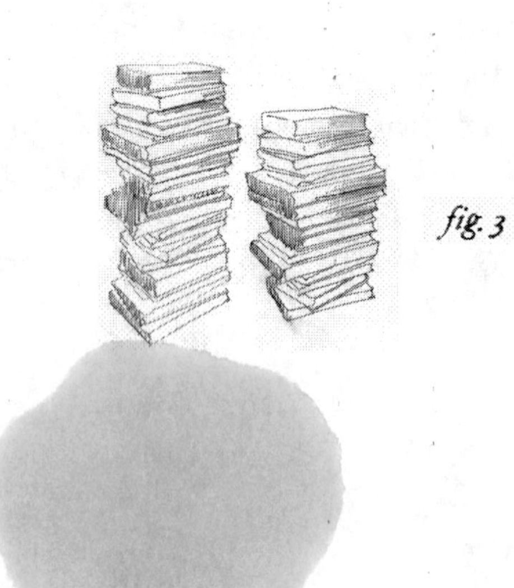

fig. 3

Acknowledgements

The author wishes to thanks the following, without whom this book would not have been possible:

The Riippi Family, Chauncey O'Neill, Carolivia Herron, Salar Abdoh, Nancy Gray, Emma Low, Chris Connelly, Ryan Davidson, Jason Cook and everyone at Ampersand, Cami Thompson, Lindsay Randall Boone, Scott Hoffman, Tammi Guthrie, Michael Poffenberger, Ashley Dabb, Brendan Kiely, Benjamin Lowenkron, Andrew Lieb, Steve Rosenstein, Melissa Broder, The Moroney Family, Dana Bos, Liz Riley, C.C. Long, everyone at The CementWorks, Tucker Hall, Donal Scott Owen, *The Flat Hat*, Housing Works Bookstore, The Cakeshop, Biddy's Pub, the members of the band Aloha, and—once again—L.